NO WAY OUT

"Where are you going? Mr. Underwood, I have to get Ethan home—his mother will be home soon and she'll be worried. . . . Mr. Underwood!"

Anger made Rebecca's voice louder than she intended, but still he paid no attention to her. He drove steadily, from time to time checking the rearview mirror and matching his speed to the other cars on the highway.

What was going on? He had to talk to her. Reaching across, she took hold of his arm. "Mr. Underwood!"

Without even looking in her direction, he took his right hand off the steering wheel and brought his closed fist down hard on her forearm. "Shut up," he muttered. "You're coming with me."

LOOK FOR THESE OTHER THRILLERS BY BEVERLY HASTINGS:

HOME BEFORE DARK . . . Sara's afraid to walk home by herself after school—because *someone* is waiting for her.

SOMEBODY HELP ME . . . Laurie was the only one who could hear the child's voice in the night, crying out, "Help me!"

WATCHER IN THE DARK . . . For Erin, being alone in the house was frightening. But realizing she *wasn't* alone was worse.

D1554465

Berkley Books by Beverly Hastings

WATCHER IN THE DARK
SOMEBODY HELP ME
HOME BEFORE DARK
DON'T WALK HOME ALONE
DON'T TALK TO STRANGERS
NO WAY OUT

NO WAY OUT

BEVERLY HASTINGS

B

BERKLEY BOOKS, NEW YORK

NO WAY OUT

A Berkley Book / published by arrangement with
the author

PRINTING HISTORY
Berkley edition / October 1994

ISBN: 0-425-14399-6

BERKLEY®
Berkley Books are published by The Berkley Publishing Group,
200 Madison Avenue, New York, New York 10016.
BERKLEY and the "B" design
are trademarks belonging to Berkley Publishing Corporation.

PRINTED IN THE UNITED STATES OF AMERICA

10 9 8 7 6 5 4 3 2 1

CHAPTER ONE

Juggling her books impatiently from one arm to the other, Rebecca glanced at her watch and then up at the big clock on the wall. Neither one of them gave her any comfort. According to both, it was already ten minutes to three, and the second hand seemed to be sweeping around the clock face much too quickly. Wouldn't Mr. Bennett ever finish going over Rob Aiken's math quiz with him? I just have one stupid question to ask, Rebecca thought irritably. Come on, hurry up!

At last Rob seemed to be gathering up his papers and preparing to depart. Before he'd even moved away from the teacher's desk, Rebecca was sitting down. "Mr. Bennett, I don't understand why my answer to question fourteen is wrong. It seems to me the result should be positive, not negative."

Mr. Bennett smiled at her. "Well, Rebecca, I

have to admit that it was a tough question—not a trick question, mind you, but a difficult one. And you certainly aren't the only person in class who got it wrong. You see, what you have to remember is that these negative numbers here indicate . . ."

As she tried to follow Mr. Bennett's painstaking explanation, Rebecca couldn't keep her foot from tapping restlessly against the chair. He was a nice person and a good teacher, but he talked so slowly! And she knew from experience that interrupting to try to hurry him along simply made things worse.

"So you see, every time you have that kind of situation, your answer has to be negative." Finally he was winding it up. "Is that clear to you now? Or do you want to go over it one more time, just to make sure?"

"Oh, no," Rebecca told him hastily, slapping the book closed and stuffing her quiz paper into her folder. "I'm pretty sure I understand now, but I'll look it over again tonight. Thanks a lot, Mr. Bennett." She flashed him a smile and then bolted for the door.

Zooming through the hall, Rebecca caught a glimpse of a small, dark-haired figure sitting on the floor near the junior-class lockers. It was her best friend, Danielle Hu, head bent as usual over an untidy stack of papers that threatened to spill out of her hands and all over the floor. "Hi, Dani!" she called.

The other girl looked up, peering through the fringe of shining black bangs that nearly covered her eyes. "Hi, Rebecca, what's up?"

"I can't stop, I'm gonna be late for work." Without slowing her rapid pace, Rebecca added over her shoulder, "Call me tonight!"

It was an easy fifteen-minute walk to the house where Rebecca baby-sat for Ethan Underwood every afternoon, but by now it was already five after three and Mrs. Underwood made a big point of Rebecca always being there without fail at three-fifteen. The bus that delivered three-year-old Ethan from nursery school rarely arrived before three-thirty, but as Mrs. Underwood said, "You never know, it might be early." Rebecca tried hard to arrive on time. She could see that it would be frightening for Ethan if no one was home to greet him after school.

As she hurried along the sidewalk Rebecca thought once again how lucky she was to have this job. True, it was sometimes inconvenient to have her whole afternoon taken up every day after school, but on the other hand Mrs. Underwood paid more than most people who wanted baby-sitters, and Ethan was a darling little boy.

When Rebecca had started this job in September, Ethan was just beginning nursery school. At first he'd been kind of scared and shy with her. But by now, three months later, he seemed perfectly happy. In fact, Mrs. Underwood had said that over the Thanksgiving break Ethan had been upset and worried because his "Becca" wasn't there.

Panting slightly, Rebecca climbed the steps to the front door and fished in her bag for the key. Her watch said three-seventeen and Rebecca grinned to herself. If she kept this up she'd be in terrific shape—Rebecca Harper, star speed-walker!

She could hear the telephone ringing as she opened the front door. Dumping her books on the table in the hall, she hurried into the kitchen. It was probably Mrs. Underwood calling, and Rebecca wanted to make sure she knew her baby-sitter was on time.

"Hello, Underwood residence."

Nothing happened at the other end of the line.

"Hello?" Rebecca tried again. "Hello?"

There was still no response, but the line seemed to be open. Something must be wrong with the connection. With a shrug, Rebecca hung up.

Still warm from her brisk walk, Rebecca took off her jacket and glanced at her reflection in the hallway mirror. The long light brown hair that nearly reached her waist was tousled by the December breeze, and her cheeks had a healthy pink glow. Unfortunately, so does my nose, Rebecca thought, and stuck out her tongue at herself.

It was almost time to go outside and wait for Ethan's bus, so when the phone rang again, Rebecca rushed to answer. "Hello? . . . Oh, hi, Mrs. Underwood."

"I won't keep you, Rebecca, because I know you have to meet Ethan, but I wanted to remind you about the story time today at the library—it's at four o'clock."

"Yes, I remember," Rebecca told her. "We'll walk

down there and—oh, Mrs. Underwood, I think I hear the bus."

Going down the front steps and waving to the bus driver, Rebecca thought, I didn't ask Mrs. Underwood if she called earlier and couldn't hear me answer. Oh, well, if it happens again, I'll tell her so she can call the phone company and get the problem fixed.

Ethan was carefully carrying a rolled-up sheet of paper, clutching it in both small hands, so Rebecca lifted him down the step from the bus to the ground. "Look, Becca, I made a picture!"

"Hey, great, Ethan. Let's take it inside and look at it." When it was unrolled on the kitchen table and its corners held down with cookbooks from the shelf, Rebecca said, "Wow, you did a nice job, Ethan. This is you and this is your mom, right?"

The child nodded vigorously. "Yeah, and this is our house, and this is a bird that needs some food."

"Your mom will be happy to see this when she gets home," Rebecca told him. "But guess what? We're going to the library for story time, so let's get ready."

How do parents survive without going crazy? Rebecca wondered as she tried to remember everything that had to be done before they set off. She gave Ethan some juice and reminded him to go to the bathroom, she put some graham crackers in a plastic bag for him to snack on as they walked to the library, she made sure he had his warm hat and his mittens—it would be colder on the way back after the sun went down. In the flurry of activity she nearly forgot to take along *Tess of the d'Urbervilles,* which she had to start reading for English class.

Ethan chattered all the way to the library about his day at school, and Rebecca smiled at his description of how two of the "big boys" had been naughty and Mrs. Walsh had said they couldn't ride on the tricycles in the play yard until they said they were sorry. At the library, she delivered him to the children's room, where a group of kids was already gathering, and then went to find an empty seat in the adult reading room.

The first few pages of *Tess* went slowly, but soon Rebecca found herself caught up in the story. It was only when several young voices from near the checkout desk broke into her concentration that she glanced at her watch. Twenty minutes to five! Story time had been over for ten minutes.

Closing the book, Rebecca picked up her jacket and walked quickly across to the children's room. It was nearly empty. A couple of grade-school girls sat at a table, and the librarian was helping a boy look up something on the computer.

Ethan must be waiting for her where a circle of low cushions on the floor formed the space for story time. But as she moved toward it, Rebecca could see that the seating area was deserted. There were no little kids curled up on the rumpled cushions.

Then she saw a familiar-looking red jacket. Rebecca picked it up—it was Ethan's, and his hat and mittens were in a little pile on the floor. So where had he gone?

The children's room of the library wasn't very large, and soon Rebecca had walked through all of it, checking all the tables and chairs and looking on the floor between the long bookshelves. There was no sign of Ethan anywhere.

Don't panic, he's got to be around here somewhere, she told herself sternly. But she could feel her heart beating faster as she approached the librarian.

"Excuse me, Ms. Thompson." When the woman looked up at her, Rebecca went on, "I'm looking for Ethan Underwood—he was at story time, and now I can't find him anywhere."

The gray-haired librarian sighed and glanced around the children's room. "Oh, dear. Mrs. Madison who does the story time seems to have left—but she usually waits for all the children to be collected when she's finished. Are you sure he didn't go home with a friend?"

Rebecca hadn't even thought of that possibility—how would she ever find him if someone else had taken him home? She didn't even know which of his little friends had been at story time. Her mouth was dry as she answered, trying to convince herself as well as the librarian. "I'm sure he wouldn't do that without telling me—he knew I was waiting for him. Besides, I have his jacket here."

Ms. Thompson sighed again. "Well, let's take a look and see where he's gotten to."

They searched the children's room again without success. Then Rebecca checked the ladies' room while Ms. Thompson knocked on the door of the men's room and then went inside. Ethan wasn't in either of the bathrooms.

Rebecca's breath was coming in quick short gulps, and she clenched her hands tightly, willing herself not to start crying. When Ms. Thompson said, "Maybe he went to look for you in the adult reading room," Rebecca could only nod in reply. She turned and walked rapidly into the big room.

Where would Ethan have gone? There was a large area with several couches and armchairs, but she could see that Ethan wasn't there. Rows of bookshelves took up much of the room, with more rows at an angle toward the back. Rebecca moved quickly up one row and down the next, hoping to see a small dark-haired child. But there were no children at all.

Emerging into the reference area, where people sat on low stools to use the computerized catalogs, Rebecca glanced toward the desk at the front of the library. Ms. Thompson stood talking to the checkout guy, who was shaking his head.

Rebecca bit her lip and began searching the reference area, even looking under the tables and behind the reference desk. At last she admitted to herself that Ethan wasn't there. What am I going to do? she thought helplessly. Glancing out the window, she saw that it was almost dark. Nightfall came early in December. What if Ethan had gone outside, somehow managing to push open the heavy doors? He'd be cold without his jacket, and he'd probably soon be terrified. Would he try to go home by himself, crossing all those streets and surely getting lost in the dark? She couldn't stand to think about it.

Near the window there was another smaller seating area, with just one couch and two big armchairs. No one was sitting in any of them, but Rebecca walked in that direction anyway, determined to exhaust every possibility.

She went around the chairs, thinking that Ethan might be sitting on the floor where he'd be blocked from view. But he wasn't there. The couch was backed against the wall, facing out into the room, but now Rebecca could see that there was a narrow space between it and the wall behind it. Hopelessly she knelt on one end of the couch and peered over the back.

And there he was! Curled up on the floor with his head pillowed on one arm, fast asleep.

"Ethan!" Scrambling off the couch, Rebecca pushed the end of the heavy furniture until it moved away from the wall. Then she quickly bent and picked up the still-sleeping child. "Oh, Ethan!"

Slowly the child's big brown eyes opened. He looked puzzled for a moment and then he smiled. "I was playing hide-and-seek from you, Becca."

She hugged him hard. "Oh, Ethan, and I'm so glad I found you!"

CHAPTER TWO

The next day after school Rebecca felt compelled to watch Ethan like a hawk. Yesterday when Mrs. Underwood got home shortly after six o'clock, Rebecca hadn't told her about losing Ethan at the library, and she felt a little bit guilty about that. But, she told herself fiercely, it definitely will not happen again!

It was a gloomy overcast day anyway, with possible snow predicted for the evening by the weather forecasters. Ethan seemed perfectly happy to stay inside and drink hot chocolate after he got off the bus. While they sat at the kitchen table, blowing gently into their mugs in an effort to cool off the cocoa, the telephone rang. Rebecca reached over to pick it up. "Hello, Underwood residence."

There was dead silence at the other end.

"Hello?" she tried again. "Hello, who is it?"

Now she thought she could hear the faint sound of an indrawn breath. "Hello, can you hear me?"

There was another long moment of silence and then a click—the caller had hung up.

Putting the phone down abruptly, Rebecca met Ethan's questioning gaze. "Who was calling you?" he asked.

Rebecca shrugged. "I don't know," she told him. "No one answered at the other end."

When the hot chocolate was finished, Rebecca got out some paper and soon Ethan was busy drawing with his colored markers. He asked her how to draw a dog and she grinned ruefully. "I'm not very good at drawing, Ethan, but I'll try."

Her creation looked more like a monster than a dog when it was done, and the bright purple marker she'd used just added to its bizarre quality. Ethan laughed when she told him it was a space dog, and he began drawing a spacecraft for her dog to ride on.

By four-thirty he was tired of markers. He wanted to watch *101 Dalmations,* his current favorite video, and while Rebecca put it in the VCR she glanced out the window. The sky was grayer and darker than before, and what looked like sleet was dripping off the trees. I guess winter is really on its way, she thought. Too bad I didn't wear boots today.

As the video began, the telephone rang again. In the kitchen Rebecca picked it up. "Hello, Underwood residence."

Once again no one answered her, but this time she could definitely hear someone breathing at the other end. Annoyed, she asked sharply, "Who is this?"

And again, after a moment, the connection was broken with a click.

Setting the receiver back in its cradle, Rebecca shivered slightly and wrapped her arms around herself. There was something very creepy about these phone calls. She hated the feeling that someone was checking on her. Whoever was calling knew where she was and could make her answer the phone whenever he wanted—somehow she felt certain it was a "he." But she didn't know who it was, and it made her feel exposed and vulnerable.

Maybe Mrs. Underwood has that service where you can punch in a special number and it will dial whoever just called you, she thought. I'll have to remember to ask her. Then she thought, But maybe I don't want to know who's making these calls. Suppressing another shiver, she went to sit down with Ethan and watch the cheerful antics of the 101 Dalmations.

When Ethan's mother arrived, her coat soggy with icy rain, Rebecca called her own mother to ask for a ride home. While she waited she told Mrs. Underwood about the two hang-up calls. "Oh, and I just remembered, there was one yesterday, too, just when I got here."

An expression that might have been alarm or dismay crossed the woman's face, but she replied briskly, "Oh, dear, that's so annoying, isn't it? But I think whoever it is will give up if you just hang up right away on any call when no one answers you."

"Well, okay, but I was wondering, do you have that phone thing where you can dial whoever just called you even if you don't know the number? Because . . ." Her voice trailed off as Mrs. Underwood shook her head decisively.

"No, I didn't buy that service when they offered it. And I don't think it's a good idea to do that anyway—it just encourages these pranksters and gives them the attention they're looking for."

Two quick beeps sounded outside and Rebecca gathered up her things. Ethan ran to give her a hug. "Bye, Becca."

"Bye, Ethan, see you tomorrow."

She ran out to the car and around to the driver's side. She'd had her learner's permit since September when she turned sixteen, and she couldn't wait to take the test and get her license. Giving Rebecca a look of humorous resignation, her mother climbed out and went around to the passenger side. As they buckled themselves in, Mrs. Harper said, "I should have known you wouldn't let me drive home, honey. But go carefully—there are some treacherous patches of ice."

Later that evening Rebecca put down her pencil. Finally she was finished with the math homework—she deserved a break! Standing up, she stretched and moved over to peer out the window. Sleet was still coming down, though it seemed to be slowing slightly, and she could see icy slush collected in the corners of the window. A nice night to be inside, she thought, and turned to survey her room.

It wasn't big, but it was a cozy haven, full of memories. The old-fashioned maple bed and matching dresser had belonged to Rebecca's grandmother, and though sometimes Rebecca wished she could redecorate in a sleek modern look, more often she enjoyed the feeling of family history the old furniture gave her. On her bookshelf were some of her childhood favorites—fairy tales, *Alice in Wonderland, The Wind in the Willows*—and stuffed in one corner, embarrassingly, her well-worn teddy bear.

There were more recent memories, too. Rebecca's gray eyes narrowed as her gaze fell on the photo that showed a grinning dark-haired guy on a beach playing volleyball. Andy—or Andrew Hollister the third, no less, she thought with a little spurt of bitter sarcasm. They'd been a couple—an item—from the middle of last year until just before school started in September. And then suddenly, with no warning, it had ended. Rebecca still didn't understand what had happened, and she'd pretended to everyone except Dani that the breakup had been her idea or at least a mutual agreement. But, she admitted to herself now, it still hurt.

The phone rang, startling Rebecca, and she picked it up quickly. After nine o'clock her parents rarely answered the phone, telling her half-jokingly that it wasn't worth it because the calls were always for her.

"Oh, hi, Dani. Funny, I was just thinking about you."

"Good things, I hope," her friend said with a laugh. "So what's up?"

"Not much," Rebecca told her, "unless you count finishing the math homework as an important late-breaking news story."

"You're finished?" Dani sighed theatrically. "I just barely started, and I got so frustrated, I had to stop and call you. I don't think I was meant to take math. But listen, I have to tell you this weird thing that happened after school. You know Joe Streeter, that big sophomore who always kind of skulks around and never says a word to anyone? Well, he and Billy Adams apparently had this thing going ever since second period when Billy took Joe's cap and wouldn't give it back or something stupid like that—you know how mean Billy can be. So after school Joe waited for Billy in the parking lot and challenged him to a fistfight. Can you believe it? I mean, it's like back in the Old West or something."

"Hey, amazing," Rebecca said. "And you're right, Billy's a creep, but Joe's a lot bigger than he is. So did Billy end up with a black eye or what?"

"No, that's the truly bizarre part." Dani paused impressively. "You're not going to believe this, or maybe you are, but Billy pulled out a knife! And then I guess a bunch of seniors who were there grabbed him and stopped the whole thing, and now it seems like Billy's going to be suspended or something. I heard all this from Al Jenkins when I was leaving after orchestra rehearsal."

"Wow!" In her deepest voice Rebecca intoned, "Violence in the high schools makes its evil presence felt in small-town USA."

Dani laughed. "Yeah, little Porterville joins the real world at last. Aren't you sorry you weren't there to hear all about it?"

"Oh, Dani, don't start. You know I need this job." Now more than ever, Rebecca thought. Her dad, who had worked for a big computer company for years, had recently lost his job, along with many of his coworkers. He was doing consulting work, whatever that was, but Rebecca knew her parents were worried.

"Yeah, I know," Dani said quickly. "Actually, I think you're lucky—Ethan's such a cute kid. What's his latest thing?"

"Oh, he's still into *101 Dalmations*," Rebecca told her. "But, Dani, this really weird thing happened today—someone called on the phone and then didn't say anything when I answered. He just listened and breathed, and then after a while he hung up."

"Oh, yuck!" Dani exclaimed. "I just *hate* when that happens—all that heavy breathing, just like in the movies."

"It wasn't actually heavy breathing," Rebecca said slowly. "It was more like he didn't want me to know who was calling. I mean, the breathing was just regular—I don't think he meant me to hear him at all."

"Well, that's almost worse!" Dani paused and then said, "Maybe it was a burglar trying to find out if the house was empty."

Rebecca couldn't repress the shudder that went through her body. "Oh, Dani, that's a horrible thought. What if he calls earlier one day and then breaks in and he's there when I open the door?"

"Just be sure to make a lot of noise getting your keys out and rattling the doorknob and stuff like that," Dani told her consolingly. "Then he'll have time to run out the back door!"

"Dani, you're great!" Rebecca laughed a little shakily. "Advice for baby-sitters, Part One!"

"Well, anyway, I don't really think it was a burglar." Rebecca realized that Dani knew the idea had scared her and was trying to come up with a more reassuring explanation. "I bet it was some guy who's in love with Ethan's mom, and he was disappointed when you answered instead of her. Or, I know, maybe it's her ex-husband and he wants to get back together with her."

Rebecca shook her head, then realized that her friend couldn't see her. "You've been watching too much talk-show TV," she said teasingly. "But seriously, I don't think Ethan's dad ever calls or visits or anything. As far as I can tell, he's out of their lives completely, and I think she wants it that way."

"Oh, really? How come?"

"I don't know, that's just the impression I get. But listen, Dani, I've got to get back to work—I have to do that summary for history and I haven't even read the chapter yet."

"Yeah, I know. I think we need a vacation. Anyway, I'll see you tomorrow."

Rebecca put the phone down and opened her history book. But she stared unseeingly at the chapter heading as she thought about her conversation with Dani. The idea that the silent phone caller was some guy who was in love with Mrs. Underwood wasn't much of an improvement on thinking that it was a burglar looking for an empty house. After all, if he didn't have the common decency to say something when Rebecca picked up the phone, he must be pretty weird. Maybe he's one of those strange guys with an obsession about a woman he's never actually met or spoken to, she thought, remembering the plots of various TV movies she'd watched. Yuck, I hope not!

Settling down to her reading, she told herself, It's probably just a wrong number—it's someone who wants the service station or the dry cleaners and isn't polite enough to apologize and say he's made a mistake. But she couldn't help hoping that whoever it was wouldn't call again.

CHAPTER THREE

On Friday at lunchtime Rebecca and Dani sat with several of their friends, making plans for the evening. The high school in the neighboring town, Dyersburg, was holding an event they called a "Sports Night." Students from Porterville were invited to come and play basketball, volleyball, floor hockey, and whatever else. As Dani said, it was an attempt to make the kids at the two schools "love their enemies." But Rebecca thought it was a good idea. "After all," she told her friends, "it's not as if I have such a fabulous social life right now—I could stand to meet some new people!"

After much discussion, they agreed that Dani would pick up Rebecca at the Underwoods when Ethan's mother got home and drive her to her house. Then Al Jenkins, who had the use of his mom's car that night, would drive the two of them and whoever else needed a ride to the other school.

As they parted to go to their after-lunch classes, Dani called, "And don't forget, if you don't wear sneakers, they won't let you in the gym!"

Rebecca grinned and waved to her friend. Turning into the stairwell, she was still smiling as she walked up to the second floor. She pushed open the heavy door that led to the hallway, and toppled forward as someone pulled it open from the other side. Clutching at the books in her arms to keep them from falling, she staggered clumsily. Strong arms caught and steadied her, and then released her just as quickly.

"You okay?" Andy Hollister's familiar voice was cool, and to her chagrin Rebecca felt herself blushing.

"Yes," she muttered. "I was just pushing open the door and—" Why was she explaining? He must realize what had happened without her going into all the details. And even worse, why was she sounding so apologetic? "Anyway, thanks for saving me from disaster," she said with an attempt at lightness.

"No problem," he responded automatically. Then he opened the door and disappeared down the stairs.

Rebecca stared after him until the door closed with a click. Her cheeks still felt hot and she knew her eyebrows were drawn together in a frown of annoyance. Why did it have to be

Andy of all people? In a small high school like Porterville's you'd think I'd run into him all the time, she thought. But Andy wasn't in any of her classes this year, and in fact she'd seldom seen him since the beginning of the school year. Was this the first time she'd actually spoken to him since the painful evening when he'd told her he "needed his freedom" or whatever words he'd used? Rebecca thought it was.

She nearly stamped her foot in frustration. All her careful plans to treat him with cool politeness hadn't done her much good. Then the funny side of it struck her, and she smiled unwillingly. I guess that's what they mean by throwing yourself into a guy's arms, she thought. Slapstick comedy, right here in the halls of Porterville High! Wait till I tell Dani.

When school was over, Rebecca jammed her books and notebooks into her backpack and hurried outside. The air was crisp, and though it was cold, the brilliant sunshine made even the bare tree branches glow. She could hardly bear the idea of going inside again, and as soon as Ethan arrived on the bus, Rebecca told him they were going to the park.

They sat on a bench in the sun while Ethan devoured the crackers and slurped the juice Rebecca had brought along. Then she pushed him on a swing. He was learning to pump for himself, but he still loved to be pushed. "Higher, Becca, higher!"

He laughed gleefully as she warned, "Hold on tight!" and then pushed him hard enough so she could run under the swing at its highest point.

When he'd had his fill of swinging, Ethan wandered over to the sandbox and soon was absorbed in building an intricate system of roads, complete with bridges made of small sticks. Rebecca sat on the bench, enjoying the quiet. No other little kids were in the park today. At the other side of the playground area four guys were playing basketball; they'd obviously been playing long enough to get warm, because their jackets lay in a heap on the grass near the basket. Rebecca squinted, wondering if they were kids she knew from school, but she didn't recognize any of them. Her gaze traveled past them to a man who stood leaning against a tree. He seemed to be staring at her, but he was too far away for her to see him clearly. Then his position shifted and she realized he must be watching the ball game.

"Becca, come here! Look what I made!" Ethan's voice was full of excited pride, and when Rebecca looked at his creation, she could see why. Half of the big sandbox was now a network of roads, rivers, and hills. Her admiration was genuine as she said, "Ethan, it's great!"

"Now I'm gonna make some more roads," he told her importantly. "But don't watch."

"Okay," she agreed. "You call me when it's done so I can come and look."

Sitting down again on the bench, Rebecca suddenly felt chilly—the sun was sinking and long

shadows stretched across the grass. She'd give
Ethan another ten minutes or so, and then they'd
head home.

The sounds from the basketball court had
changed, and when she glanced that way, Rebecca
saw that the game was over. As she watched, the
four players exchanged a few words with one
another and then, jackets slung over their shoulders, they sauntered toward the bench where she
sat. Something about the way they walked made
her uneasy. Trying to ignore the hollow feeling
in her stomach, she scolded herself—Don't be an
idiot, it's broad daylight, they're just walking over
to the gate on this side of the park.

"Yo, little mama, what's up?" They had halted
in front of her bench and the one who had spoken stood looking straight at her and combing his
longish wavy dark hair with his fingers.

Rebecca looked away, but the four of them
blocked her view of anything else. They were
older than she'd thought, maybe in their early
twenties.

"Yo, mama, I'm talkin' to you. What's yo' name?"
He was obviously trying to sound tough and cool.
Rebecca began to feel frightened, as he meant her
to. She tried to decide what was the best thing to
do—ignore them and say nothing? Or answer his
question politely but coldly?

"She ain't got no name, man," one of the oth-
ers said.

"Nah, she got a name. Maybe she just too cold
to talk."

"Yeah, she cold all right." That was the first one again. He was obviously the leader, and he was enjoying his power. "Maybe you guys should warm her up a little, keep her from freezin' out here."

Nobody moved for a moment, and then two of them sat down on the bench, one on either side of Rebecca. The one on her right draped his arm casually along the back of the bench. Rebecca didn't look at him, but she could feel her skin crawl with awareness of his presence.

The silence stretched out, heightening the tension between Rebecca and the dark-haired guy. By now she was not only scared but angry. She certainly wouldn't give him the satisfaction of answering his remarks, even if she could trust her voice not to shake. She shifted her gaze, trying to see past them. Where was the man who had been watching their basketball game? If he was still in the park, surely he'd come and help her if she screamed.

"Becca?" The little voice sounded uncertain.

Before she'd even thought about it, Rebecca responded, "Yes, Ethan." It came out in a strangled whisper. She cleared her throat and said again, louder, "Yes, Ethan, I'm coming."

Her words seemed to dissolve the frozen tableau she and the four young men had been trapped in. The fourth one, who hadn't said anything before, now muttered, "Aw, come on, let's go."

The guy on Rebecca's left stood up quickly, but the one on the other side lingered. She felt him touch the nape of her neck as he gathered a handful of her waist-length hair. "Mmm, nice," he said softly as he let it slide slowly through his fingers.

Rebecca shuddered uncontrollably and her eyes met those of the dark-haired guy who still stood facing her. An unpleasant smile creased his features. "Later, sweet thing."

Then they were gone, jostling each other as they walked toward the park gate and throwing loud phrases and laughter back and forth.

Rebecca stood up abruptly, the remains of her anger and fear mixing with a feeling of deep humiliation that nearly made her stumble and fall. She'd been so scared—and of what? A little nasty teasing, that was all it had amounted to. And she'd acted so helpless and feeble! She still didn't know what she should have done to stop them. But as she walked toward the sandbox, she admitted to herself that she'd been right to be frightened— the aura of menace that had enveloped her had been real.

Ethan stared up at her with troubled eyes. "Becca?"

Swiftly she dropped to her knees and put both arms around him. "It's okay, Ethan." She held him close. Looking over his head, she saw the man who had been leaning against the tree. As she watched, he turned away and walked quickly toward the far gate.

CHAPTER FOUR

All weekend the incident in the park stayed in Rebecca's mind. Though she tried hard to keep from thinking about it, a mental image of the dark-haired young man's face appeared whenever she wasn't concentrating, and the creepy feeling of the other guy's hand caressing her hair made her shudder. The whole thing had left her feeling dirty. In fact, she'd made everyone impatient waiting for her on Friday night because she'd simply had to take a shower and wash her hair before going to the Sports Night.

She'd wanted to tell Dani about it; she felt certain that sharing it with her friend would make it less frightening. But every time she'd started to describe it, the words wouldn't come. Somehow she couldn't bring herself to talk about it. It would mean revealing how completely helpless and ashamed she'd felt.

She hadn't done anything—she'd just sat there and let things happen. Maybe if she had stood up and told them to get lost, they would have left her alone. Or maybe not—but she hadn't even tried. She squirmed when she remembered how she had just sat there like a rabbit caught in oncoming headlights, frozen in fear.

Her wish to put the whole incident out of her mind was so strong that she couldn't even consider taking Ethan to the park on Monday, though it was another sunny day. But on Tuesday she lectured herself firmly as she walked to the Underwood house after school. *Are you going to let a bunch of creeps run your life and dictate where you will or won't go in your own town?* she demanded silently. *Don't be such a baby!*

While Ethan was having his snack, Rebecca looked out the window. The sky was gray and overcast, and she wondered if this might be the last dry day before another sleeting rain or even a snowstorm moved in. That decided her, and she said to the little boy, "Let's go to the park, Ethan. We can check and see if your city in the sandbox is still there."

When they stepped outside, the air felt colder than she'd expected. *Maybe this isn't such a great idea,* Rebecca thought. But Ethan was already telling her that he wanted to go on the swings again, "really high!" With a mental shrug of her shoulders, Rebecca closed the door behind them.

Walking into the park, Rebecca couldn't help scanning the playground area and especially the basketball court. With relief she saw that today the park wasn't completely empty. Two young women sat chatting on the bench while two little girls who looked about six or seven years old bounced up and down on the seesaw. The women must be nannies, Rebecca thought; they were older than she was, but not old enough to be the girls' mothers. A group of boys—she recognized one of them as her friend Hannah's brother in seventh grade—were playing football, their game punctuated by a lot of shouting and laughter.

Feeling absurdly grateful for the protection of other people's presence, Rebecca pushed Ethan on the swing. I love to hear him laugh like that, she thought with a rush of affection. He's such a nice kid.

After a while he was ready for something different. Rebecca watched as he tried a few other pieces of equipment, all the time circling nearer and nearer to the big slide. It was old—Rebecca remembered sliding down it when she was a small child—but still sturdy. She knew Ethan was a little bit afraid to go down it, and she waited for him to climb the ladder on his own. At the top he sat holding on to the rail.

"Want me to catch you, Ethan?" she called, walking to the bottom of the slide.

The child nodded and waited for her to get in position. Still he hesitated for a moment or two, and then with a deep breath he let go of the rail and pushed off.

The slide was fast, and Ethan flew into her arms with a solid impact. The tension had left his face, and his eyes sparkled while his mouth opened in a wide grin. "I wanna do it again!" he cried.

Rebecca smiled back at him. "Okay, I'll be waiting for you," she told him.

She watched as he climbed carefully up the ladder and once again paused after sitting down at the top of the slide. Then, this time with a smile of delight, he launched himself down the slippery metal channel.

Again Rebecca caught him, and he laughed happily, proud of his daring. As she set him down, a voice spoke from behind her.

"Hello, Ethan."

Startled, Rebecca turned. A man dressed in jeans and a brown parka stood there, his face shadowed by a hunter's cap with earflaps turned up and the brim pulled low on his forehead. She wondered for a moment if he was the same man who had stood watching the basketball game last week. But she couldn't tell—she hadn't gotten a close look at that man, and lots of people had brown jackets.

Ethan was standing perfectly still, the smile wiped from his face. At last the man said quietly, "Aren't you going to say hi to me, Ethan?"

Still staring at the man, the child murmured, "Hi," so softly that Rebecca could hardly hear it.

The man looked at Rebecca. His voice was courteous but oddly formal as he said, "I'm Ethan's father—Harley Underwood. And you must be . . ."

"Rebecca Harper." The words came out in automatic response as her brain tried to take in what he'd said. Ethan's father! What was he doing here? Somehow Rebecca had always assumed that he lived far away from Porterville, maybe in another state. She had never seen any indication that he visited Ethan or even kept in touch with him. Certainly the child never talked about him, and the few times Mrs. Underwood had mentioned him, she'd given Rebecca the impression that her ex-husband was out of her life for good.

Mr. Underwood was gazing intently at Ethan, but his expression was unreadable beneath the brimmed cap he wore. The three of them seemed immobilized, as if time had stopped for a moment. Then the man said, "Well, Ethan, I've come to take you out for some hot chocolate. Wouldn't you like that?"

The little boy didn't answer, and the man said, "Come on, let's go." He reached out to take the child's hand.

Ethan seemed to shrink away from him slightly, and when the man took a step toward him, the boy moved quickly to Rebecca. He stood pressed up against her with one arm wrapped around her leg.

Was Ethan afraid of his father? Rebecca wondered. It was hard to tell, but he didn't exactly seem fearful—just cautious and kind of shy. But that's not surprising, Rebecca thought, if he hasn't seen his dad very often.

Then a more disturbing thought flickered across her mind. Was this man really Ethan's father? The little boy wasn't giving her any clues about whether he recognized the man or not. And how would I know if this guy is Mr. Underwood? Rebecca wondered. Ask to see his driver's license?

No, she thought, that whole idea didn't make sense. He called Ethan by name, and he knew the child's last name was Underwood. Of course he was Ethan's dad.

"Come along, Ethan, I don't have a lot of time." Mr. Underwood's voice held impatience now, and he took another step toward his son. Ethan's arm tightened around Rebecca's leg as he stared at his father.

"Mr. Underwood, I don't think—" Rebecca broke off. She couldn't think of a way to tell this man that his son didn't seem to want to talk to him without making it sound like an insult. She started over. "I mean, I can't let Ethan go anywhere without checking with his mother first. Um, you see, I'm responsible for him and . . ." Her voice trailed off again. And what? And I can't let him go and get hot chocolate with his own father? She couldn't say that—it sounded ridiculous.

Rebecca saw Mr. Underwood's mouth tighten. He must be annoyed, and no wonder. "I'm glad you feel responsible for my little boy, Miss Harper." His words were icy cold. "But I've driven a long way to get here to spend a short visit with my son, and I don't have time to waste discussing it with you."

He bent toward Ethan, his arms extended to pick up the little boy. Instinctively Rebecca put her hand on Ethan's shoulder, and the child turned, burying his face in the fabric of her jeans and clinging to her leg with both small arms.

Mr. Underwood straightened, and Rebecca thought, He's really angry now. What should I do? She looked toward the bench where the two young women had been sitting. But they were walking toward the gate now, chatting busily while the little girls raced ahead of them. Quickly Rebecca glanced around the park. The boys playing football had moved farther away and were now yelling happily as they piled on top of one another in a tangle of arms and legs. There was no one else in the park. And even if someone had been there, how would that help Rebecca handle this awkward situation?

When he spoke, Mr. Underwood's voice was quiet and even. "It seems Ethan doesn't feel entirely comfortable with me. I haven't seen him for quite a while—that's why I'm here. I guess the best thing will be for you to come with us, Miss Harper." He gestured toward the gate near the basketball court. "My car is right over there."

Relieved, Rebecca nodded. If she went with him, Ethan wouldn't be nervous or scared. And her problem of not wanting to let the child go off with someone she'd never met, while feeling bad about not letting him spend time with his own father, would be resolved. She bent down and gently released Ethan's arms, taking one of his hands in hers. "Come on, Ethan, we're all going to go and get hot chocolate with your father, okay?"

The boy didn't answer, but he walked along willingly at her side. As they got into Mr. Underwood's light brown car, Rebecca pushed aside a wisp of nagging uneasiness. I'll be glad when this is over with, she thought. I don't think I like Ethan's dad very much.

Mr. Underwood started off away from the park, but he didn't turn left toward the main street of Porterville. As he drove straight through the intersection, Rebecca looked at him in surprise. But of course, she thought, he probably doesn't know the area. "Mr. Underwood, you should have turned left—there's a place that has hot chocolate and stuff right in town."

"I know where there's a better one," he told her curtly. He hadn't looked at her as he spoke, and Rebecca sank back against the seat, her uneasiness flickering to life again.

They drove in silence and Rebecca stared out the window, wondering where Mr. Underwood was taking them. At the far edge of Dyersburg, he turned left on a road that paralleled the New York Thruway, and Rebecca realized that they must be heading for the Dunkin' Donuts a mile or two farther on. It was farther than she'd thought they would be going, but at least now she knew their destination.

At four-thirty on a Tuesday afternoon, the

Dunkin' Donuts shop was completely empty except for the teenage boy behind the counter. Rebecca didn't really want hot chocolate, but it seemed easier not to make a fuss. She and Ethan sat at a table against the wall while Mr. Underwood went up to the counter to order. The teenager filled the three mugs with a bored expression and then went back to the rear of the store, where he sat singing under his breath along with the radio.

Mr. Underwood stood at the counter with his back to Rebecca and Ethan, fumbling with the mugs. Maybe he's having trouble carrying all three mugs, Rebecca thought. But before she could go over to help, he turned around and brought the steaming mugs to the table.

While Rebecca carefully sipped her cocoa and reminded Ethan that it would be very hot, Mr. Underwood watched them and occasionally asked Ethan a question. But they were mostly questions that seemed inappropriate for a three-year-old— things like "Do you like football?" and "What are you learning in school?" For the most part they sat in awkward silence. Mr. Underwood, who drank his hot chocolate quickly, acted almost impatient for Ethan to finish. Rebecca, too, couldn't wait to get out of there and take Ethan home.

The longer they sat, the more uncomfortable Rebecca felt. Briefly she thought of calling to see if her mom was home and asking her to come pick them up. But the idea of explaining this to Mr. Underwood and facing his certain annoyance while she waited for her mother to arrive seemed worse than just driving back with Mr. Underwood, which would at least get this over with faster.

At last Ethan slurped the last few drops of his cocoa, and Rebecca wiped his sticky hands and mouth with a paper napkin. Mr. Underwood stood up. "Ready to go?"

Rebecca nodded quickly. She helped Ethan back into his jacket and zipped it up for him, then picked up her purse. As they emerged into the parking lot, she realized for the first time that it had begun to snow. The small icy flakes were already piling up in uneven lines against the Dunkin' Donuts building, and the outside tables were covered with a thin layer of white that sparkled in the glow of the streetlights. Maybe this snow will stick, she thought, instead of melting as soon as it hits the ground. Maybe school will be canceled tomorrow.

"Look how pretty the snow is," she said to Ethan, trying to coax a smile from his solemn face. But he just gazed briefly at the light dusting that obscured the windshield of his father's car. Then, without saying a word, he climbed again into the backseat and sat still while Rebecca fastened his seat belt.

Mr. Underwood started the car and activated the windshield wipers. After waiting for a break in the traffic, he pulled out of the parking lot. But rather than going left, back the way they had come, he turned right and headed north.

"Where are you going? Mr. Underwood, Ethan has to go home." Rebecca's voice was sharp with annoyance.

Glancing briefly at her, he said, "A different way back—easier in the snow."

Still annoyed, Rebecca thought, What a wimp! The road, traveled by plenty of cars at this hour, was kept clear of snow by so many tires—it stretched ahead of them, wet and shiny. But at least, whichever route he took, they didn't have far to go. The uncomfortable outing had gone on more than long enough, and she couldn't wait to say good-bye to this man who didn't even seem to be enjoying his visit with his child. Mrs. Underwood should have told me about this, she thought crossly. But she realized that probably Ethan's mom hadn't known that her ex-husband was coming to see Ethan. I'll tell her about it when she gets home, Rebecca decided, and she can tell him not to do it again.

At an intersection Mr. Underwood stopped for the red light. Rebecca didn't know this section of the road very well, but surely he should be turning left here to get back to Porterville. Why wasn't he in the left lane? As she started to point out his mistake, he turned right and then quickly turned left. Gathering speed, he drove up the on-ramp to the Thruway.

Outraged, she turned to him. "Where are you going? Mr. Underwood, I have to get Ethan home—his mother will be home soon and she'll be worried. You have to get off at the next exit and drive us back to Porterville!"

By this time Mr. Underwood's car had merged into the traffic stream. He ignored her words, staring out through the windshield with a frown of concentration.

"Mr. Underwood!" Anger made Rebecca's voice louder than she intended, but still he paid no attention to her. He drove steadily, from time to time checking the rearview mirror and matching his speed to the even fifty-five miles per hour of the other cars on the highway.

What was going on? He had to talk to her. Reaching across, she took hold of his arm. "Mr. Underwood!"

Without even looking in her direction, he took his right hand off the steering wheel and, before she could draw her own hand back, brought his closed fist down hard on her forearm. "Shut up," he muttered. "You're coming with me."

Stunned, Rebecca stared at his profile. Fear began to send icy tentacles down her back as the word *kidnapped* forced itself into her mind. The rhythmic swish of the windshield wipers was the only sound inside the car as it sped north through the darkness.

CHAPTER
FIVE

Rebecca slumped in the passenger seat of Mr. Underwood's car, staring out the side window without focusing on anything they passed. The car heater was on, but Rebecca had never felt so cold. Her hands and feet were stiff, like blocks of ice, and every now and then an uncontrollable shiver made her whole body tremble.

Her mind, too, felt numb. Images tumbled through it helter-skelter—scenes from movies and TV shows about kidnappers and mad killers, scenes of innocent victims leaping from speeding cars, scenes of car crashes and bloody death. But her brain was too sluggish to grab hold of any of these pictures or to make sense of what was happening to her. How could she possibly be in a car with a little kid and his father whom she'd never met before, zooming along the New York

Thruway with no idea where he was going and no way to make him turn back and go home? Her brain rejected it—it didn't make sense. But sense or not, it was obvious that Ethan's father wasn't planning to take them back to Porterville.

The car slowed and Rebecca roused herself to pay attention. They were approaching the Tappan Zee Bridge that crossed the Hudson River, and although there was no toll for cars going west, the traffic lost speed as the lanes merged. She stared at the man in the car that was for the moment keeping pace next to Mr. Underwood's. A middle-aged man with a mustache in a sporty-looking white car—maybe she could get him to help her. But as Rebecca raised her hand to wave and attract his attention, he sped up and zipped into a space that had opened in front of Mr. Underwood's car.

Energized by the possibility of getting help from the occupants of another car, she gazed purposefully out the window, willing someone to stay alongside long enough to notice her. But in a very short time it was clear that it wasn't going to happen. She had never realized before how isolated people were in their cars. The drivers kept their eyes on the road in front of them, peering through the snowflakes that swirled in the beam of the headlights. It was as if the people in the other cars didn't exist for them.

Discouraged, Rebecca leaned back in her seat again. Now that she thought about it, she wasn't sure what she would have done if she had been able to attract another driver's attention. Open

her window and yell that she and Ethan were
being kidnapped? Someone in another car would
never hear her in the wind created by the cars'
speed. And besides, all Mr. Underwood would have
to do would be to speed up or drop back so the car
and its driver were no longer next to Rebecca.

Could she write a message and hold it up to the
window? She dismissed the idea almost before it
formed in her mind. For one thing, she didn't
have her notebook with her—it was back at
Ethan's house, and there was nothing bigger
than a Kleenex in her purse. And for another,
in the dark nobody would notice her note or be
able to read it if they did see it, and meanwhile
it would be obvious to Mr. Underwood what she
was trying to do.

Large green-and-white signs flashed past, an-
nouncing town names like Nyack and Congers
and telling drivers the distance to the Garden
State Parkway. Rebecca hadn't traveled on the
Thruway frequently and she had no idea where
Mr. Underwood might be going. A wave of panic
twisted her stomach, but she pushed it away with
an effort. She had to think of some way to get
away.

Maybe she could open the door of the car and,
choosing a moment when Mr. Underwood slowed
down, jump out and roll to the edge of the road.
Despite her anxiety, a sarcastic smile curved
Rebecca's lips. Oh, right, she thought, it'll be
the start of a fabulous career as a Hollywood
stuntwoman. Get real, Rebecca, you'd just end

up with a million broken bones if you even lived through it—and if you could get up your nerve to jump in the first place.

Then a shock of realization struck her like a smack in the face. Even if she figured out a way to jump out of the car without hurting herself, she couldn't do it—she couldn't leave Ethan behind. Whatever was going to happen, Rebecca was still responsible for him.

He'd been so quiet—Rebecca wondered if he'd fallen asleep. Turning, she peered over her shoulder into the backseat. He wasn't sleeping. He sat perfectly still, his eyes wide and dark, gazing solemnly into her face.

She gave him a small smile, but his expression didn't change. He looked so lonely, all by himself back there. Forcing herself to smile at him once more, she settled back into her seat.

She wondered what Ethan was thinking. Was he frightened? Did he realize that his father was taking him and Rebecca somewhere without anyone knowing about it? Did he want to go with his father or was he wishing for home and his mom? Rebecca didn't know.

I'd better concentrate on how to get both of us away from Mr. Underwood, she thought. It wasn't easy to keep her mind focused. She seemed to be drifting off into a fog, and her eyelids felt heavy. Maybe she could just close her eyes for a moment to rest them.

With a clunk, Rebecca's head banged against the cold window of the car, and she jerked awake.

What's the matter with me? she thought. How can I be sleepy at a time like this? Get your act together, Rebecca, and think! Was there a tollbooth coming up sometime soon? She couldn't remember, but she thought that when she'd gone to Albany once with her mom, they had had to stop somewhere to pay a toll. So, assuming that the car would have to stop sometime at the toll plaza, wherever it was, how could she use that stop to escape?

Stealthily Rebecca felt for the buckle of her seat belt. She had to be able to open it quickly, whenever a chance of escape presented itself. Satisfied that she could get out at a moment's notice, she tried to plan what she could do then. When Mr. Underwood stopped to pay the toll, he'd have to open his window. But there might not be time for Rebecca to call out to the toll taker and explain what was happening. Mr. Underwood would just speed off before she could make herself understood.

And what if it was an automatic tollgate, with no person there to talk to even if she could make herself heard? Rebecca's heart sank, but she refused to give up. Doggedly she considered the possibilities. At last she decided that as soon as the car stopped in the tollbooth, she would jump out and run around to stand in front of the car. Surely Ethan's father wouldn't actually run over her. He'd have to stay stopped in the gate. And she could shout for help while she stood there—even with automatic lanes, there was always at least one tollbooth with a live person in it for people who didn't have change.

Alert now, Rebecca stared straight ahead, straining to see the tollgates appear in the distance. Taillights glowed fuzzily, their gleam diffused by the snow that was falling faster now. The highway's surface was still clear, but slush was beginning to build up along the edges, and the grass beside the road was covered with a thin blanket of white.

The silence in the car was oppressive, and as the minutes dragged by, Rebecca felt drowsiness creeping over her again. She opened her window about an inch and breathed in the cold air that flowed over her face, hoping it would wake her up. But suddenly the window went up again, closing off the stream of air from outside. Startled, Rebecca realized that Mr. Underwood must have a set of window controls on his side of the car. She looked across in time to see him stare briefly in her direction before looking back at the highway. He didn't have to speak—the message was clear: He would make all the decisions.

At last Rebecca saw the big yellow sign she was waiting for: TOLL BOOTH 1 MILE, CARS 40C. Adrenaline flooded her body as she prepared herself for action. There weren't many other cars on the road, and she wouldn't have much time. Her hands found the buckle of her seat belt, and she turned to look at the door of the car. It was locked. She'd have to be very quick to make sure she got the lock unfastened and the door opened in time to run in front of the stopped car.

She wiggled back in the seat, sitting up straight and staring at the approaching tollgate, her hands now clenched on her seat belt. Activated by the control, the driver's window opened without a sound, and a blast of cold wind reached across the seat. The car slowed gradually, aiming left toward one of the automatic unmanned lanes that stood empty. As it pulled between the lane dividers, Rebecca unfastened her seat belt, muffling its click with her hands. Then, hoping that Mr. Underwood wouldn't look her way, she reached for the door's lock with one hand and the handle with the other.

The car stopped and Rebecca pulled the lock button up. But before she could open the door, the lock snapped back down again. Rebecca looked at Mr. Underwood, hearing the coins he had flung into the bin clattering through the toll machine. She reached for the lock button again. "Don't do it," the man said without so much as a glance in her direction. The gate went up and the car went through, skidding slightly as it picked up speed.

Staring at his profile in the car's dim interior, Rebecca thought, He knew I was planning to jump out and stop him—that's why he relocked the door so fast. She felt overwhelmed by the certainty that this man—her enemy, as she now thought of him—could see inside her mind and block every move she made. For the first time since the whole nightmare began, she felt she might burst into tears. But her pride wouldn't let her. Averting her face, Rebecca stared out her window into the passing darkness.

Only a short while later—Rebecca wasn't sure how much time had passed—a small voice spoke from the backseat. "Becca?"

"Yes, Ethan?" He sounded so forlorn! Poor little guy, he must be pretty scared. Rebecca twisted around in her seat and looked back at him.

"I need to make pee-pee."

"Okay, Ethan, hold on and we'll stop very soon." She looked at Mr. Underwood, who didn't seem to have registered what his son had said. "We have to stop," she told him, "so Ethan can use the bathroom." Still he didn't react. "Mr. Underwood," Rebecca insisted, "please get off at the next rest area. Ethan has to—"

"I heard you," the man said, his voice cold and without inflection.

The car sped along in silence once again. Rebecca's brain was churning. This would be her chance—why hadn't she thought of it before? Whatever rest area they stopped at, there would be people—at the gas station, at the gift shop and the fast-food counters. And there would be phones. She just had to figure out what would be the best and surest method of escape.

Feverishly Rebecca ran through all the possibilities she could think of. If Mr. Underwood let her take Ethan into the ladies' room, that would be perfect. She'd find some responsible-looking woman inside and explain what was happening. She'd ask her to telephone Rebecca's parents and Mrs. Underwood—Rebecca would give her some change or tell her to call collect and use Rebecca's name so they'd be sure to accept the charges. Better yet, she could ask the woman to find a policeman or some official person, and she could stay inside the ladies' room with Ethan until that person arrived to help her. The best part was that Mr. Underwood couldn't pursue them into the ladies' room without causing a lot of commotion.

But what if he took Ethan into the men's room instead? If that happened, surely Rebecca would have time to find a cop or someone who could help her while she waited for them. She thought, I can hide out in the ladies' room to slow him down. But no—she was afraid the man would simply leave her there and take Ethan wherever he was going, and she knew she couldn't abandon the little boy. She would just have to be quick and persuade whoever was available to help her. Whatever I have to do, she thought, Ethan and I won't get back in this car.

The thought raised her spirits immeasurably, and she began to rehearse what she would say. Impatiently she tapped her fingers against her leg and glanced at the dashboard clock. It was only a few minutes after six, though Rebecca felt it ought to be at least midnight, she felt so tired. Never mind, the whole horrible business would be over very soon.

A few minutes later the welcome words REST AREA AHEAD appeared on a sign at the right of the roadway. As the car slowed, Rebecca stared to the right, looking for a building with light pouring out through plate-glass windows. But there was no building. In dismay Rebecca realized that this was a pull-off parking area with no services, and only a couple of dark cars at the near end.

The parking lot hadn't been cleared, and Mr. Underwood drove cautiously along the roadway, his tires making crunching noises in the snow. He kept going until he reached the far end, just before the road led back onto the Thruway. There were no other cars nearby. Choosing a spot away from the streetlights and under the thick branches of a bare oak tree, he pulled in to the curb and turned off the engine.

In the total silence he turned to stare at Rebecca. "Miss Harper, I want you to listen carefully." There was no emotion in his voice, and Rebecca shivered—it was like the voice of a dead man. "I will help Ethan go to the bathroom out here, under that tree. You will get out and stand next to us. You will not go anywhere else and you will not try to stop any car that might happen by. If you do, I assure you that Ethan and I will be in my car and gone faster than you can believe possible. I don't wish to leave you behind, but make no mistake—I will if I have to. And without your presence, Ethan will be very unhappy and might even hurt himself accidentally. I'm not very experienced with little boys."

Long before this speech was over, Rebecca had given up. She sat with shoulders slumped, chilled to the bone by the man's words and the way he

said them. How stupid she'd been to think he'd
pull into a big rest stop, with a building where
there would be people to help her. It had been
crazy to imagine that she'd be able to get away,
and take Ethan with her, so easily. Wake up and
smell the coffee, she told herself bitterly. You'll
have to come up with something a little cleverer
than that.

As she stood next to Ethan in the snow, she
gazed toward the cars whose headlights lit up the
highway as they passed. There were people there,
and help just for the asking. But, Rebecca thought
dully, there's no way to get to them. Ethan and I
are trapped—there's no way out.

CHAPTER SIX

Marian Underwood cautiously climbed up the steps to the front door, holding the banister so she wouldn't slip in the snow. She'd taken a taxi from the Porterville train station, hoping to save her shoes from getting soaked, but as she tried to find her key she could feel the wet cold already seeping through the thin leather soles.

At last she got the door open and stepped inside. Odd—there were no lights on anywhere.

"Ethan? Rebecca? I'm home!" Kicking off her shoes and listening for the happy sounds of her son coming to greet her, Marian padded into the living room and switched on the lamp next to the couch. The house remained completely silent.

Frowning slightly, Marian stood at the foot of the stairs and called again. "Ethan? Come on down here, honey, I'm home!" When she heard no answering sounds, she walked up the stairs and into Ethan's bedroom. Maybe he and Rebecca had both fallen asleep. But there was no one in her son's room or in any of the other rooms on the second floor.

Marian felt a small flutter of panic that made her breathe a bit faster. She pushed it down firmly. Probably Rebecca had taken Ethan to a friend's house. No doubt she had left a note on the kitchen table.

But when she turned on the kitchen lights, there was no note to tell her why her child and his baby-sitter weren't home. Where had they gone? The beginning edge of fear was making her heart beat rapidly, but Marian refused to acknowledge it. There had to be some perfectly good explanation for why they weren't here when she arrived home from work— though Marian told herself that she'd have a few firm words to say to Rebecca about *always* letting her know where she went with Ethan. It was surprising—Rebecca was usually so responsible.

Suddenly she thought, Maybe something happened and Rebecca had to go home to her house, and she took Ethan with her. Her finger was already punching in Rebecca's phone number before the thought was completed.

"Hello, Mrs. Harper? This is Marian Underwood. I just got home and Ethan and Rebecca aren't here, and I was wondering if they were at your house, or if perhaps you know where they are."

Rebecca's mother sounded puzzled. "Why, no, they aren't here, and I haven't talked to Rebecca this afternoon, so I don't know what she planned to . . ." Her voice trailed off uncertainly.

"Oh." The disappointment hit Marian like a fist in her stomach. "Well, I guess I'll call some of Ethan's friends. They probably went to someone's house and haven't realized how late it is. But if you hear from Rebecca, please ask her to call me right away."

"Oh, of course," Ellen Harper replied quickly. "I can't understand it. It isn't like Rebecca. I think I'll call and see if her friend Dani knows where Rebecca is. But I'm sure she and Ethan will be arriving at your house very soon, and when they do, will you tell her to call me?"

"Yes, I will." Marian Underwood hung up abruptly. It wasn't reasonable, but she couldn't help feeling annoyed that Rebecca's mother didn't know where her daughter was. Marian had counted on finding Ethan safely at the Harpers' house. And the concern she had heard in Ellen Harper's voice had only served to give substance and validity to her own fear.

Walking around the house, Marian methodically turned on every lamp, noticing with a shiver how dark it had grown outside. She found the list of phone numbers of the children in Ethan's nursery school. As she carried it into the kitchen, it rattled slightly and she realized that her hands were trembling. Picking up the phone again, she punched in a number. While she waited for someone to answer, she thought, Please let Ethan be there.

In her own kitchen a few blocks away, Ellen Harper turned off the stove burner under the pot of water she was boiling for noodles. She picked up the telephone to call Dani. When she had explained that Rebecca wasn't at the Underwood house and asked if Dani had any idea where she had gone, the girl answered quickly, "Gosh, no, Mrs. Harper, as far as I know she went to Ethan's house right after school like she always does. And even if she took him someplace, like the park or the library or something, she'd be back by now—I mean, it's dark and it's snowing pretty hard."

Ellen tried to control the unsteadiness in her voice as she replied with determined cheer, "Yes, I'm sure they'll turn up any minute. Thanks, Dani, and if you hear from Rebecca—"

"Oh, sure, I'll tell her you're looking for her if I see her, Mrs. Harper."

Hanging up, Ellen gazed blankly at the wall while a series of nightmarish scenarios chased each other through her head. What if Rebecca had taken Ethan to the playground and the child had gotten hurt falling off a swing or something? They might be at the emergency room of the local hospital. Even worse, what if they'd been crossing a street and a car had skidded in the snow and hit one, or even both, of them? Her daughter might be seriously injured or unconscious—Ellen refused to let herself think that Rebecca might be dead.

She knew that this was nothing but horrific fantasy, that it was far more likely that Rebecca had lost track of time and would walk into Ethan's house any minute, full of apologies for being late. But once she'd let these dreadful imaginings in, she was unable to banish them from her mind. Ellen wished that Bob was home. Her husband was a calm rational person who didn't get excited without good reason, and she yearned for his comforting presence. But he had taken the car to go for a job interview, and she wasn't sure what time he would be back, especially with the snow.

It's much too soon to panic, Ellen told herself. Everything is sure to be all right. But after another moment of staring unseeing at the wall, she had to do something. Should she call some of Rebecca's other friends to find out if she and Ethan had gone to see them? Even before she had formulated this idea, Ellen rejected it. Rebecca simply would not have gone anywhere without letting Mrs. Underwood know where she was—her mother felt absolutely certain of that—and it wasn't likely anyway that she would take a three-year-old to visit one of her high-school friends.

Nervously Ellen drummed her fingers on the kitchen counter. She opened the refrigerator and stared into it, then closed it without taking anything out. Turning on the cold water in the sink, she filled a glass, took two swallows, and poured the rest out. She couldn't seem to think of anything useful to do, but she couldn't sit still either.

Finally, reluctantly, she decided to call the local hospital where accident victims were taken if they were picked up by an ambulance or the police. The police! That was a better idea. She knew that it would be hard to get information from the hospital's emergency room, but if something had happened to Rebecca or Ethan, the Porterville police would know about it. And they weren't total strangers. In fact, Joe Delarra who had recently joined the department was the son of Ellen's good friend Kathy Delarra—the two families had shared picnics and holiday parties over the years. Hoping Joe was on duty, she picked up the phone. When someone answered, she said, "Joe Delarra, please."

After several clicks and hums he came on the line and she plunged into her story, explaining that Rebecca had a regular after-school baby-sitting job for Ethan and that nobody seemed to know where the two of them were. "And, Joe, you know Rebecca, you know she's not an irresponsible kid, she wouldn't go off somewhere without leaving a message for Mrs. Underwood. And maybe you think I'm getting hysterical without enough information, but I really believe something must have happened, an accident or something like that, because it's the only reason I can come up with why she hasn't come back from wherever she went." Ellen stopped to take a deep breath. She found she was close to tears; putting her fears into words had made them more real to her.

Joe was talking and she composed herself to listen. "Yeah, Mrs. Harper, I can understand how you must be feeling. But we already got a call from Mrs. Underwood about this, and she asked us to check the hospitals and all. We made some calls, and we found out the ambulance here in Porterville wasn't called, and the emergency room at St. Anne's doesn't have any record of Rebecca or the little boy—Ethan—being brought in there. We're gonna keep in touch with them, but so far it doesn't look like either of them got hurt."

He paused and said something to another person at the police station, but Ellen couldn't understand what it was. Then he came back on the line. "I was just checking with Jim here on the switchboard, Mrs. Harper. He sent one of the cars up to Raglan Drive where the Underwoods live and they're gonna be taking a look all around there, in the playground and along all those streets in that area. It's not the greatest weather for it, but they're out looking now, I think, and we'll let you know the minute we hear anything, if we do."

He paused again, and Rebecca's mother said quickly, "Oh, Joe, thank you."

"That's okay," he replied awkwardly. "And Mrs. Harper, try not to worry. The most likely thing is she went to someone's house when it started snowing and she just lost track of time. I bet she's on her way home with the kid right now."

"Thanks, Joe, I hope you're right."

Ellen Harper hung up the phone and sat unmoving in her kitchen. She hoped desperately that Joe Delarra was right—that Rebecca had been thoughtless enough to take little Ethan to someone's house and not get in touch with his mother. Or with me, she thought dully. She must know that I'd be worried, too. Groping for possibilities, no matter how farfetched, she thought, Maybe the phone isn't working at this person's house. Or maybe she was getting a ride home and the person ran out of gas.

But Ellen knew with cold certainty that these were vain hopes, born of her fervent wish that nothing awful had happened. A heavy lump settled in the pit of her stomach, and the tears she'd held back until now spilled down her cheeks. Oh, Rebecca, sweetheart, where are you?

CHAPTER SEVEN

Back in the car and out on the highway again, Rebecca's feeling of being trapped intensified. Mr. Underwood hadn't let her sit in the backseat with Ethan, though he'd relented enough to give her a blanket from the trunk to wrap around the little boy. It wasn't as comforting as sitting back there with her arm around him, Rebecca knew—and she admitted to herself that the human contact with a child cuddling up against her would have made her feel better, as well as Ethan. With a spurt of anger she thought, What did Mr. Underwood think I could do from the backseat—strangle him and let the car go off the road? Not very likely! But he obviously feels he needs to have me under his eye at all times.

The failure of her plan to escape at the highway rest area had been a heavy blow to Rebecca. It was clear that any further efforts to get away would have to wait. But wait for what? It was too terrifying to let her imagination drift over the uncertainties—where they were going, what would happen when they got there, what Mr. Underwood planned to do with them, whether anyone knew yet that they were gone, and most mysterious of all, why Ethan's father had decided to kidnap his son and Rebecca in the first place. The answers that surfaced in her mind were too awful to think about. Rebecca tried to make her brain a blank, to simply stop thinking at all for the time being. She closed her eyes for a moment.

Sometime later Rebecca realized that the car was pulling away from a tollbooth. She must have fallen asleep—how could she? Now she felt disoriented, not sure how long she'd slept or how far they'd driven. She hadn't been soundly asleep the whole time, she was sure—she remembered glimpses of buildings along the highway and other cars they had passed.

The dashboard clock read nine forty-five. They must be a long way from Porterville, Rebecca thought hopelessly. She felt chilled and depressed, and suddenly frightened as the car fishtailed in a skid on the narrow road they had taken away from the tollbooth. She clutched at the dashboard as Mr. Underwood controlled the skid. Then she glanced into the backseat. Ethan was wedged in the corner, his head pillowed on part of the blanket he'd scrunched up under his cheek.

Grateful that the boy was still asleep, Rebecca peered out her window. Snow covered the ground in a thick layer like frosting on a cake. Tree branches were edged in white, each tiny twig outlined and defined by brilliant softness. At any other time Rebecca would have exclaimed at the beauty of these winter woods, but now she wished it would all melt away. Because Mr. Underwood was driving too fast, and she was scared.

The two-lane road curved abruptly and traced a path up and down hills and around shadowy shapes that might be barns or outcrops of rock. In the pitch dark the car's headlights made wavering tunnels through the snowflakes that fell thicker and faster than ever. They passed no other cars, and the tire tracks on the road ahead of them were almost invisible, nearly filled in by the snow that had accumulated since that last vehicle went by.

Under the covering of snow the road must be slippery and icy. Rebecca could feel the car sliding sideways on the curves, as if its tires couldn't get enough traction. She wanted to ask—no, tell— Mr. Underwood to slow down before he skidded off the road. But when she looked across at him, she decided it would be better to keep quiet.

He was peering intently through the windshield, his head pushed forward on his neck as if getting closer to the glass would help him see. His mouth was moving, and every now and then Rebecca caught a few words. She knew that whatever he was saying wasn't addressed to her. But maybe she could pick up a clue to his plans. She stared

out her window again, her ears straining to catch
what he was saying.

"It's not fair, not right . . . make her pay, make
them all pay, for what they did . . . see how she
likes it . . . they'll pay, all right, but it's too late
now. . . ."

The car skidded again, and righting it seemed
to require Mr. Underwood's undivided attention,
because he stopped talking to himself. But Rebecca
had already heard more than she wanted to. She
huddled against the door, frozen with dread. Mr.
Underwood must be talking about Ethan's mother—that was the *she* who he wanted to make pay
for whatever it was she did to him. Probably he
wanted to make her pay for taking away his son.
Cases like that were in the newspapers all the
time, when parents who didn't have custody kidnapped their own children and took them away
into hiding.

But if that's what was going on—if Mr. Underwood planned to hide out with Ethan and change
their names and all that—why had he brought
Rebecca along? It didn't make sense to do that.
So maybe he was planning to hold Ethan for ransom, hoping to make his ex-wife pay in a different way.

Gingerly Rebecca considered this possibility.
Was he planning to hold her for ransom, too? How
was he going to set it up? Visions of suitcases full
of cash being thrown off a bridge or out of a train
window appeared before her inner eye. Then the
thought that had been knocking insistently at her

brain broke through. If Mr. Underwood intended to hold Ethan and Rebecca for ransom and then let them go, he'd been pretty stupid about it. They knew who he was and what he looked like and could certainly identify him if he got caught afterward.

She couldn't keep her mind from following this thought to its logical conclusion. Mr. Underwood would have to kill both of them to make sure of his safety after getting the ransom money. And killing Ethan was what he meant when he talked about making his former wife pay.

He must be crazy, Rebecca thought bleakly. He's going to kill both of us, and it's all my fault. The melodramatic words echoed in her head, but they didn't really make much impression on her. She didn't feel terrified and she wasn't about to cry. She just felt empty.

Mr. Underwood was muttering to himself again, but Rebecca didn't bother to try to understand him. What was the use? Even when the car slid around a corner onto a still narrower road, she sat without moving. Her head ached dully and she still felt groggy from sleeping all that time in the car. She was thirsty, too. Vaguely she noticed that this new road was buried under a smooth layer of snow. No vehicles had traveled it, at least not lately. In fact, the only way to tell where it went was to follow the lines of trees along its edges.

Thank goodness, Mr. Underwood was driving more slowly now. Time passed as if in a dream.

After a while Rebecca noticed that Mr. Underwood seemed to be looking for something at the side of the road. A mailbox? A sign? She didn't see anything out of the ordinary at the spot where he turned and drove rapidly up a long steep track that wound between huge evergreens.

At the top he finally stopped, his headlights illuminating a wooden house. Rebecca could see a door under the wide overhang that apparently formed a primitive porch in front of the house. In the cleared space sat a heavy wooden table and two chairs, all of them rimmed with a thin dusting of snow. The pillars supporting the overhang were tree trunks still covered with bark, giving the small building an old-fashioned rustic look.

Leaving the headlights on, Mr. Underwood got out of the car. Rebecca watched as he hunched his shoulders against the swirling flakes and trudged through snow that was already up to his ankles. At the door of the house he paused. Now Rebecca noticed a wooden sign, obviously handmade, nailed to the wall next to the door. She squinted to read what it said: CROCKETT'S CABIN.

Mr. Underwood had reached up and was moving his hand carefully along a ledge that jutted out slightly over the door. He must be looking for a key, Rebecca deduced, and soon she was proved correct. He paused and then brought his hand down carefully. Standing to one side of the door so the lights shone directly on it, he fumbled for a moment at the lock and then pushed open the door.

Immediately he pulled it almost closed again to keep out the wind-driven snowflakes. Shuffling back to the car, he got in and, without a word to Rebecca, began rummaging through the glove compartment. He found a small flashlight and took it back to the cabin, stamping his feet at the doorway before he disappeared into the darkness inside.

As he vanished, Rebecca thought, Now's my chance—I should take Ethan and run. But she knew it wouldn't work. By the time she gathered up the sleeping child and set off down the winding track, the man would be out of the house. He could easily catch up to them, and she didn't want to think about what he might do if he got angry.

Automatically Rebecca glanced at the house, whose doorway was still lit by the headlights' beams. The headlights! Maybe the keys were still in the ignition!

Checking, she saw the key ring dangling at the side of the car's steering column. Quickly she looked again at the house. Mr. Underwood had not reappeared, but Rebecca knew he couldn't be in there much longer—she didn't have much time.

Scrambling across into the driver's seat, she found she couldn't reach the pedals. Now frantic with the need for haste, she felt under the front of the seat for the lever that would release it. After what seemed like endless minutes she finally found it and let out her breath in relief as she jerked the seat forward.

Now she'd have to start the engine and turn the car around before Mr. Underwood could rush out of the cabin to stop her. It was impossible to tell in the darkness and snow how much clear space there was for a turn. Still, if other cars had driven up here, it couldn't be too difficult to do. She'd back the car around to the right, where the ground looked fairly flat in front of the house, and then turn hard left as she went forward. Rebecca prayed that the car's turn would clear the trees— if she had to back up again to get herself pointed down the hill, she'd probably run out of time.

She looked over her shoulder into the backseat. Ethan was still sound asleep, scrunched up in the corner with the blanket up to his chin. What would happen if Rebecca tried to escape in the car, and failed? If Mr. Underwood stopped her before she got away with Ethan, what would he do? He might take out his anger on her—he'd already hit her once in the car. But even worse, he might punish Ethan instead. Rebecca didn't think she could stand that.

She put out her hand toward the key, and then drew it back. Maybe she should wait for a better opportunity to escape, one with more certainty of success. Perhaps it was better if she went along with Mr. Underwood now, so he wouldn't be watching for an attempt to get away. If he was lulled into a false sense of security, he might be more likely to let her and Ethan go.

Suddenly Rebecca saw the inconsistency of these ideas. It didn't matter if Mr. Underwood thought

she was being cooperative or not, he wasn't going
to drop them off in the nearest town and give them
money for a phone call. She'd have to stop dithering
about all the things that could go wrong and just
do something.

Taking a deep breath, Rebecca told herself,
Okay, this is it. But as she reached again for
the key in the ignition switch, Mr. Underwood
stepped through the doorway of the house and
marched purposefully in her direction.

Rebecca stared at him in dismay. It wasn't fair!
She'd had a chance to get herself and Ethan away,
and now the opportunity was gone. Dully she
watched him approach the driver's side of the
car and open the door.

She could tell he was surprised and displeased
to find her sitting there. "What are you doing?"
he asked roughly.

What could she say? She couldn't let him think
she'd tried to escape. Rebecca felt certain that
arousing Mr. Underwood's suspicions would be
the worst thing she could do. Clutching for an
answer, she dropped her gaze to the dashboard.

"The heater," she said quickly. "It's cold—I
wanted to turn on the heater." She hoped it
sounded convincing. The lie had leaped off her
tongue before she'd even thought.

Mr. Underwood stared at her for another
moment. Then he said abruptly, "Get inside."
Without waiting for her to move, he opened
the back door and began to unfasten Ethan's
seat belt.

Rebecca hesitated until she saw Mr. Underwood pick up his son and lift him out of the car.
Then she located her purse and stepped out into
the snow. The heavy wet flakes immediately coat-
ed the sleeves of her jacket and caught in her
eyelashes. Before she'd gone three steps she could
feel the cold dampness seeping in through the
seams of her boots and chilling her feet. She was
wearing the leather boots she'd gotten for her
birthday—elegant soft tan leather, not meant for
bad weather. She'd put them on that morning
when the weather had been clear. It seemed so
long ago—Rebecca felt she could hardly remember that morning and the comforting, regular routine of getting up and going to school.

She stepped through the doorway and saw that
while Mr. Underwood had been inside—while she
had tried fruitlessly to get away—he had found
and lit some candles. Their flickering light showed
her a large room that extended all the way to the
back wall of the cabin. At that far end Rebecca
could see a fireplace with sturdy furniture grouped
around it. Near the door, to her right, was a solid
wooden table and four chairs. There was a wide
doorway in the wall to her left, and she could
make out two more doors, both closed, farther
along that wall.

Mr. Underwood stepped into the room, stomp-
ing the snow off his sneakers, and carried the
child in his arms to the couch in front of the
fireplace. Setting Ethan on the cushions, the man
turned and squatted, taking a log from the pile

beside the hearth and beginning to lay a fire. Rebecca moved quickly to the couch and sat down, peering to see whether Ethan was awake.

His eyes, shadowed in the candlelight, stared gravely into hers. Overwhelmed with an emotion that combined fear and sadness, she pulled his small body onto her lap. Ethan was still for a moment. Then he burrowed closer to her and she sat with both arms wrapped tight around him, gazing unseeingly at the stone chimney while Mr. Underwood built the fire.

CHAPTER EIGHT

Half an hour later Rebecca's eyelids were drooping. She'd never been so tired—she felt she could barely move. She had sat motionless on the couch with Ethan until the fire, now blazing high, warmed the cold room. Then she had taken off her jacket and helped Ethan with his.

Meanwhile Mr. Underwood had moved energetically around the cabin. Rebecca hadn't paid much attention to what he was doing, but eventually he called to her.

"Bring Ethan—it's time to eat."

It took enormous effort to stand up, but when she did, Rebecca saw that he had put some kind of food on the table near the front door. She carried Ethan over there and sat him in one of the chairs. By the light of the candle on the table, she looked at the three bowls of unidentifiable stuff.

"What is this?" Her voice sounded flat and rusty from lack of use, and her mouth tasted funny.

"Pork and beans," the man told her shortly. "It's all there is here." He gestured to the open doorway that led to the kitchen and gave a brief laugh. "Beggars can't be choosers."

Tentatively Rebecca took a spoonful, and nearly spat it out. The food was cold, with a greasy thick quality that was totally unappetizing.

Mr. Underwood watched her. Then he said, "I can't turn on the propane until morning when it's light enough to see it, so we can't use the stove or the hot water. There's no cold water either, until I can find the main and turn it on tomorrow." He gestured to the glasses he had placed in front of Rebecca and Ethan. "That's soda."

It was the most he'd said at one time to Rebecca, and she roused herself to take advantage of his willingness to communicate. She had to try to learn as much as she could about their situation. She took a drink of the orange soda in her glass. It was pretty disgusting, but obviously it was the only liquid the place had to offer. "Is this your house?" she asked.

The man shook his head mockingly. "Oh, no," he told her, "it belongs to a friend. And he doesn't know I'm here. No one knows. . . ." His voice trailed off, and then he looked at Ethan. "Eat your supper, Ethan. You must be hungry."

His words made Rebecca realize that, appetizing or not, pork and beans was all they were going to get tonight. And it wouldn't help if she and Ethan didn't eat—underneath her lethargy she was determined that they'd escape from this place the first chance they got, and they needed to be strong enough to do it. Forcing herself to take another spoonful, she smiled at the little boy. "It's okay, Ethan, go ahead and eat it. It's like camping-out food."

The child took a few bites, but soon his head was nodding and his spoon dropped to the floor. Rebecca gathered him up and had started to take him back to the couch when Mr. Underwood stopped her.

"Not there—in here." He opened the farthest of the two closed doors and carried a candle into the room. Two sets of bunk beds and a low chest between them took up most of the space. The room was cold, and Rebecca was glad to see several blankets folded at the end of each bed.

Ethan kept drowsing off and it took Rebecca quite a while to get him ready to go to sleep in one of the lower bunk beds. When he was finally tucked in under layers of blankets, he didn't want her to leave. Clinging to her hand, he whispered, "I want to go home, Becca."

Her heart contracted with pity for this little boy who had been so quiet and uncomplaining up until now. He must be terrified and totally bewildered, and Rebecca was his only link with the familiar comfort of home. She stroked his forehead while she tried to think of something reassuring to say.

At last she leaned over and told him softly, "I know you want to go home, Ethan, but we can't do that right now. But we're going to have fun here—it's like an adventure in the woods and we're the explorers." The child gazed at her solemnly and she thought, He's not fooled by that, and I don't blame him. She hugged him close and said, "Go to sleep now and I'll see you in the morning."

His body stiffened in panic. "Where are you going to sleep?"

"Right there." She pointed to the other lower bunk. "I'll be here in this room all night."

Rebecca sat on the bed with Ethan until his eyes closed and his fingers loosened their clutch on hers. As she stood up she realized that she might as well go to bed herself. She certainly didn't want to sit in the other room with Ethan's father, and she still felt exhausted in spite of having slept in the car.

Should she keep her clothes on or take them off and sleep in her underwear? This question seemed extremely important and she spent a long time debating it. In the end she decided to undress; Mr. Underwood probably wouldn't come into the bedroom and she couldn't bear the thought of wearing the same clothes all of today and through the whole night and again all day tomorrow.

Blowing out the candle, Rebecca crawled into bed and shut her eyes. But now she couldn't seem to turn off her brain. Thoughts tumbled one after the other through her head: How are we going to get out of here? Will anyone figure out what happened? What is he going to do to us? Worst of all was the thought that kept coming back: It's all my fault. If I had just taken Ethan home from the park, if I hadn't gotten in the car with him . . .

Angrily she told herself, *If* isn't going to do you any good. You're here now, what's done is done, don't waste time wishing you had done things differently. Just try to come up with a way to escape.

But she couldn't keep from berating herself and wishing vainly that she could turn back the clock and start over. Turning over on the lumpy mattress, she felt tears trickling from the corners of her eyes. Then she heard a tentative little voice. "Becca?"

"Yes, Ethan?" She tried hard to sound calm and normal—she couldn't let him know she was crying.

"Becca, I'm scared. Can I sleep in your bed?"

Poor baby, she thought, of course he's scared. Aloud she said, "Sure you can, honey. Can you find me in the dark?"

He didn't answer, but in a moment or two she could feel him standing next to her bed. Pushing back the blankets, she helped him crawl in. His body felt so small and vulnerable, and she put her arm around him as he snuggled close against her. Her last thought as she drifted into uneasy sleep was, Somehow I've got to get him away from here.

When she woke up and opened her eyes, Rebecca was nearly blinded by the brilliant light at the small window of the bedroom. Climbing carefully out of bed so she wouldn't wake Ethan, she padded across the cold floor and peered outside. It must have snowed for most of the night, she thought. Bright sunshine sparkled on the unbroken layer of glistening white that covered the ground in gentle drifts. Beyond the flat expanse of snow was thick woods—evergreens whose branches, laden with heavy snow, swept down to touch the ground, and leafless trees, maybe maples or oaks, with towering frames and wide branches outlined in thick white icing. Nothing was moving. Perhaps even the birds and squirrels stay warm and cozy in their nests after such a snowstorm, Rebecca thought.

Then a sound from the other room jolted her back to the present and the horrible situation she and Ethan had landed in. She listened carefully while yanking on her jeans and sweater. She had draped her socks over the end of the upper bunk the night before, but they were shapeless and bulging and felt cold when she pulled them over her feet.

Adjusting the blankets over Ethan's shoulders, she felt a pang of affection and sympathy. Then, mentally squaring her shoulders, she walked out into the other room.

Logs were blazing cheerfully in the fireplace and Rebecca could hear the sound of running water. At the doorway to the kitchen she stopped, and Mr. Underwood turned to look at her. "The water is on, but it won't be hot for a while," he said. "And the propane is on, so you can cook some breakfast for Ethan and yourself."

Rebecca shuddered slightly. His words were perfectly ordinary, even polite, but his voice held no expression whatsoever. What was going on in his head? She had no idea.

After a moment she nodded and then turned to go into the bathroom. She winced as she splashed ice-cold water on her face and rinsed her mouth, but it was definitely an improvement on orange soda. She swished another mouthful of water and spat it out. The peculiar taste in her mouth that she'd noticed last night was still with her.

When she came out, the man was waiting for her. "I'm going to get firewood from the shed," he told her. "You stay inside. Do you understand?"

He gazed fixedly at her until she replied, "Yes." Then he walked out the door, closing it firmly behind him.

It was only after he'd gone that Rebecca realized something important—he was wearing heavy boots that laced up the front. He didn't have those last night, she thought, remembering the wet prints left by the soles of his sneakers on the wooden floor. And he didn't have those heavy gloves, either.

Hurriedly she gazed around the room. Maybe there was a collection of bad-weather gear somewhere in the house. If she could find it, she might be able to take some stuff that would be useful when—she refused to think *if*—she and Ethan got away.

No likely storage place jumped to her eye, however. And now Rebecca began to wonder where Mr. Underwood had gone. What shed was he talking about? It was frustrating not to know what lay outside the boundaries of this little cabin. She moved to the window in the side wall of the living room and saw tracks in the snow leading out of her field of vision. But from the other window in that wall, the one closer to the fireplace, she could see by craning her neck a substantial-looking shed off to her left. As she watched, Mr. Underwood emerged from it with an armload of logs and walked toward the door of the cabin.

Quickly Rebecca went into the kitchen. Somehow she didn't want the man to know she'd been spying on him. Opening the two upper cupboards, she found plenty of dishes and mugs and plastic glasses, as well as a supply of paper towels and napkins. But apart from an ancient bottle of soy sauce and a pair of salt-and-pepper shakers, the only food was canned pork and beans—at least eight large cans. They must have had a special on that stuff at the local market, she thought absently as she closed the cupboard and looked around the kitchen.

When Mr. Underwood entered the cabin, he found her opening a drawer that held silverware and kitchen stuff like a can opener, a spatula, and a couple of knives. Standing in the kitchen doorway, he stared at her until the back of her neck prickled and reluctantly she turned to face him. "I'm going outside again," he said, still in that dead-sounding voice. "You stay here." Again he waited for her nod of understanding before he went back out the front door.

This time, though, he turned to his right and Rebecca saw him pass by the kitchen window. She watched him walk steadily away from the cabin and disappear into the woods.

Now was her chance! Rapidly Rebecca tiptoed into the bedroom and picked up her boots, now stiff and hard from yesterday's walk through the snow. They're wrecked already, she thought, jamming her feet into them and reaching for her jacket. Glancing out the kitchen window, she saw no sign of Ethan's father. She hurried to the cabin door.

Rebecca drew in her breath sharply as the clear cold air hit her. Standing beneath the overhang, she gazed around. There was the car in front of the door, though the curving drive down to the road was buried in snow. Still, it was worth a try. She hurried toward it and bent to peer through the driver's window. But there were no keys in the ignition.

Rebecca's shoulders sagged in disappointment. I guess he's not that stupid, she thought dejectedly. Looking back at the cabin, she could see now that it stood in a small clearing. Around it in every direction the trees grew thick and tall, shutting off any view there might have been from this hilltop. She couldn't even see very far down the drive; the trees that lined it on both sides formed an impenetrable screen at the first curve.

Was the drive the only way to get to the cabin? Maybe there was a path through the woods. Rebecca felt an urgent need to find out, to know what possibilities of escape might be available. Trying to stay in the footprints Mr. Underwood had made earlier, she walked quickly around the cabin in the direction of the shed. The trees at the edge of the clearing, beautiful with their tracery of white, made an unbroken wall. She couldn't see an opening anywhere that might be the start of a path used by hikers or neighbors—if there were any neighbors.

Was there anything behind the shed? Her feet felt wetter and colder with every passing second, but Rebecca had to know as much as she could about this isolated place where she and Ethan were trapped. She glanced quickly across the clearing, but saw no sign of Mr. Underwood in the trees at the other side.

The snow had drifted against the walls of the shed, and Rebecca made a wide circle around it. At the back the shed looked less sturdy. The boards that made up its walls were loose in places, their ends sticking out into the air. The trees were closer here, and Rebecca could see that it might be possible to walk between them, though she didn't see anything that looked like a real path.

And that was all there was to see. The cabin, the shed, and the woods that encircled them. Deflated, Rebecca thought, What did you expect— the yellow brick road? Realizing that she'd better get back inside before Mr. Underwood returned, she retraced her steps around the shed—and stopped dead.

He was standing in front of her, so close she had almost run into him. His face under the brim of his cap looked coldly angry. They stared at each other for a long moment that seemed to stretch interminably. And then, faster than Rebecca could react, his gloved hand shot out and hit her across the face.

Gasping with shock and pain, Rebecca staggered slightly. Before she could think about running away from him, the man's other hand grasped her long hair at the back of her neck and twisted hard. "Inside!" The word hissed through the frigid air.

Stumbling awkwardly with her head forced back at an unnatural angle, she was marched back to the cabin and shoved inside ahead of him. Tears of pain and anger smarted in her eyes as he gave her hair one last hard twist and then let her go. Her feet felt numb with cold and Rebecca sank onto one of the wooden chairs around the table and tried to pull off her sodden boots. She couldn't look at him, but there was no escape from his voice.

"I told you to stay inside. I expect you to do what I say. Next time you disobey me, I won't be so forgiving." He stopped for a moment. When he went on, his voice was full of mockery. "Were you trying to get away? Now you've found out there's no way to do that until I decide you can leave. Remember that, Miss Harper."

As he walked into the kitchen, Rebecca brushed the tears from her eyes and then cautiously felt her cheek where he had hit her. It was sore and tender to her touch. She looked up to find Ethan staring at her from the door of the bedroom. His silence was so unlike him; at home he'd be chattering about whatever was going through his head, and the contrast brought new tears to Rebecca's eyes. As she beckoned to him she thought despairingly, *His father is right—there's no way out of here.*

CHAPTER NINE

The morning passed in a kind of hazy blur for Rebecca. She warmed some pork and beans for breakfast for Ethan and for herself; then, after testing to make sure there was hot water, she took a quick shower in the rusty metal shower stall and gave Ethan a sponge bath. The hot water tank was so small that she was afraid they'd run out before they finished, but she couldn't bear not to get clean as soon as she had a chance.

Afterward she tried to think of things to do to keep Ethan busy. He was still being unnaturally quiet and he stuck close to her side all the time. But he joined her in a game of pick-up-sticks using kindling twigs from the basket near the fireplace, and then Rebecca in a flash of inspiration taught him a game she'd played with Danielle when they were little. It was called Hot Lava, and it involved constructing a pathway around the whole room from chairs, cushions on the floor, and whatever else they could find. The object of the game was to travel around the pathway without touching the floor (the hot lava). Obviously Ethan didn't quite understand what hot lava was, but the jumping and climbing was a wonderful way to release some of his pent-up energy.

Mr. Underwood spent much of the morning outside. Rebecca wasn't sure what he was doing, but when he came in she glanced out the door and caught a glimpse of the car propped up on a jack. He must be putting chains on the tires, she thought. Maybe we're leaving. That hope sustained her as she told Ethan several stories—thank goodness for fairy tales, she thought as she launched into "Little Red Riding Hood."

Later she was startled to hear the coughing and then the high-pitched whine of an engine starting up. Rushing to the window, she saw Mr. Underwood riding a tractor-style snowplow. Its noise went on for a long time, and Rebecca decided that he must be plowing the drive down to the road. Maybe we really are going to leave here, she thought. Briefly she felt excited, her mind flooded with images of home and safety. Then, like a dousing of cold water, another thought crept into her brain: If we leave, he won't take us home, he'll just take us somewhere else. She wasn't sure which would be worse—to stay here or to be taken to another hiding place.

At lunchtime, stirring another pan of the inevitable pork and beans, she searched the rest of the kitchen, hoping this time to come across some paper and a pencil so Ethan could draw. She found a stub of broken pencil but no paper and was about to give up when she opened the cupboard under the sink and discovered something much more valuable. In a jumbled heap were what looked like two pairs of boots and some heavy work gloves, along with a bunched-up tangle of fabric that she thought might be a jacket.

Elated, Rebecca was about to pull out the boots when she heard the front door open. Quickly she shut the cupboard and stood up. Was he going to tell them to get ready to leave? Ethan, who had been watching her as she searched, grabbed hold of her leg and pressed himself against her.

But the man ignored both of them. He opened a drawer and took out a hammer and a handful of long nails, which he stuck in the pocket of his parka. Without a word he went back outside. Rebecca turned off the stove and began to ladle beans into two bowls. Mr. Underwood suddenly appeared outside the kitchen window, making her jump. Soon a loud pounding filled the cabin. Her heart sinking, Rebecca watched as he nailed a wide board across the lower part of the window. The kitchen seemed to get darker as he nailed another board across the top half. Enough light still came through the glass, but the boards reminded Rebecca forcefully that she, and Ethan, were prisoners.

As Rebecca sat at the table and tried to coax Ethan to eat, she heard more pounding from the bedroom and then saw Mr. Underwood hammering outside the windows in the living room. Puzzled and anxious, she racked her brain to figure out why he was doing this. It can't be anything good, she thought with foreboding. Her fears were realized when he came back inside.

Staring at her and speaking in that toneless voice she'd come to hate, Mr. Underwood said, "I'm going to get some food—and other things. You will stay here." He gestured toward the window. "Since I've learned that I can't trust you, I have nailed all the windows shut. And I will double-lock the door from the outside when I leave. So it will be useless for you to try to escape."

He was going to lock them in! Rebecca's flesh crawled at the idea, and as he turned to go she said desperately, "Don't lock the door! Please— what if there's a fire? We won't be able to get out."

Mr. Underwood looked back at her and bared his teeth in a mirthless grin. "That's right, you won't. So you'd better keep everything under control."

Her hand to her mouth, Rebecca stared after him as he went out the door. She heard the click as he turned the dead bolt. Then she listened to the car's engine starting up and the crunch of the tire chains on the snow.

Trembling slightly, Rebecca gazed blankly at the door. Though she and Ethan had been trapped in the cabin before, somehow the idea that they were now physically unable to get out made her feel far worse. She clenched her hands into tight fists and forced herself to smile as she turned to look at Ethan. His head was down on the table and his eyes were closed.

He's sleeping an awful lot, Rebecca thought in surprise. She wondered if the strain of being here in this cabin, away from his mother and home, was so exhausting for him that he needed more sleep than usual. Carrying him into the bedroom and putting him in bed, she almost envied his ability to escape into oblivion for a while. But it was worrying. Ethan didn't normally sleep so much of the day.

Neither do I, she thought, but last night in the car I could hardly keep my eyes open, and in fact I was sound asleep and didn't even see which exit we got off at. It's pretty strange that I would do that. Slowly she let other memories filter into her brain—her thirstiness, the unpleasant taste in her mouth, the headache that had nagged her all morning. What if Mr. Underwood drugged us somehow? Maybe he put something in that hot chocolate—it was the only chance he would have had.

It sounded awfully melodramatic when she put the idea into words, but it made a horrible kind of sense. And now she recalled how he had stood at the counter in the Dunkin' Donuts—was that when he'd added some kind of sleeping pill to their drinks?

The more she turned the idea over in her mind, the more convinced she was. It was a scary thought. Obviously whatever drug Mr. Underwood had used hadn't done Rebecca any permanent harm, but what about Ethan? He was sleeping so much—was the drug still in his system?

In the living room Rebecca dropped onto the couch and stared into the glowing logs in the fireplace. Still thinking about Ethan, she wondered again how he felt about his father. He didn't seem to be deathly afraid of the man, but now that she thought about it, Rebecca realized that Ethan never spoke directly to his father. Stranger still, Mr. Underwood rarely spoke directly to his son.

You'd think he'd want to get to know his own child, Rebecca thought. I mean, if he doesn't even want to talk to him, why in the world did he kidnap him? It's as if he doesn't care anything about Ethan—he acts like he's just doing a job. And what kind of father would drug his own son?

Without warning, the fleeting idea she'd had yesterday in the park popped full-blown into her head. What if Mr. Underwood isn't Ethan's father? What if he's not really Mr. Underwood? With mounting horror Rebecca realized that she had only the man's word for it that he was related to Ethan. The little boy never called him Daddy or acted as if he knew him at all. He doesn't know him, Rebecca told herself, his dad's been gone almost since he was born.

But if he's not Ethan's father, who is he? She put her hands to her temples as if she could stop the wild spinning in her brain. Did Mr. Underwood hire someone to kidnap his child? Or is this guy a total stranger? No, she thought, he has to know something about the family—he must have some connection. But surely a child's own father would care more about him than this man cares about Ethan.

As if conjured up by this thought, an image of Rebecca's father sprang into her mind. Tears slid slowly down her cheeks as she imagined how terrified and frantic her parents must be right now. Their only child had vanished from the park yesterday afternoon—nearly twenty-four hours ago. They must be beside themselves, thinking she was dead and her body would be found in some deserted wasteland. And they might be right, she thought as the tears flowed faster.

Thinking of her parents and home led to other images—of Dani, who would be as worried and upset as Rebecca's family. Dani was at school right now, going to class, wondering what could possibly have happened to her closest friend. Oh, Dani, I wish you were here, Rebecca cried silently. I wish I weren't all by myself in this horrible place!

A sound—of something brushing? scraping? on something else—froze her into immobility. Then a second sound, a heavy thud, made her clutch convulsively at the slipcover of the couch. What had made those noises? Had Ethan fallen out of bed? Rebecca rushed into the bedroom. But the child was sleeping soundly under the blankets, his mouth slightly open and his face flushed.

Back in the living room, Rebecca stood still, her ears strained for the slightest sound. And soon she heard it—a subdued rustling. It seemed to be coming from the kitchen. Rebecca's heart was thumping so loudly now that she felt it would drown out any other noises in the cabin. She forced herself to take a step toward the kitchen, though what she really wanted to do was run into the bedroom and hide under the covers.

Come on, she told herself sternly, go in and see what's making that noise. It's probably just snow sliding off the roof or something. But these brave words didn't convince her heart to stop pounding in her ears. At last she moved quietly to the woodpile next to the fireplace. Bending, she chose a sturdy stick and tested its strength against her thigh to make sure it wouldn't break at the first blow. Then, armed with this club, she walked quietly to the kitchen doorway.

The small room was completely empty. Rebecca was the only moving object in it. She walked to the window and peered out between the boards. No branches were near enough to rub and rattle against the window—of course, she'd already known that. And she couldn't see any new piles of snow that might have been loosened by the sun to slide in a rush off the roof. In fact, she couldn't see anything that might have made any noise at all.

But there had been noises. She had heard them, and she wasn't totally crazy—at least, not yet. She had to find out what had made them or she'd be nervous and jumpy all the rest of the day, and she definitely didn't need that. She'd looked in the bedroom, the living room, and the kitchen. The only place left was the bathroom.

Her heart was no longer threatening to jump out of her chest, but Rebecca still clutched her stick hard as she walked silently toward the bathroom. She tried to joke with herself—maybe the shower stall gave up the ghost and collapsed—but she couldn't summon up much of a smile. Outside the closed door she paused and then thought impatiently, Oh, for goodness' sake, Rebecca, get it over with.

She reached for the knob and opened the door—and then stood stock-still in amazement. A tall skinny black teenager who looked no older than Rebecca herself was standing on the toilet seat, his arms raised over his head toward an open trapdoor in the ceiling. His brown eyes, wide with astonishment and dismay, held Rebecca's gray ones for a long moment. Then he let out his breath in a long sigh. "Now I got trouble."

CHAPTER TEN

Rebecca stared at the boy while she tried to absorb the shock of his presence. She couldn't believe he was real—but of course he was, a real live teenage kid who had appeared as if by magic in this remote cabin where she was trapped. At last she said to him, "What are you doing here?"

Still holding Rebecca's gaze with his own, the boy shrugged and said, "Been sleeping up there." He gestured over his head and Rebecca glanced up again at the trapdoor, which now was closed. She hadn't even noticed it before. It must lead to an attic—large enough for a person, if this boy had been sleeping there. But what was he doing here?

"How did you get in here?" Her voice was sharp as she blurted out her question and she saw a wary expression settle over his face. He shrugged again and said nothing, continuing to watch her cautiously.

Suddenly Rebecca realized that he was worried. He must have broken into the cabin somehow and he was afraid she would turn him over to the police. She nearly laughed out loud—this guy must assume that she belonged here, maybe that her parents were the cabin's owners. She had to explain the real situation and get him to help her. But there was so much to explain, she wasn't sure where to begin.

"Listen," she said quickly, "I don't care how you got in. I just want to find a way to get out of here. Come in the other room—are you cold? There's a fire going. And I don't want to wake up Ethan."

The boy now looked both wary and confused, and Rebecca knew that she'd been babbling and not making much sense. Still, he jumped down lightly and followed her into the kitchen, where their voices would be less likely to awaken Ethan from his nap. His eyes fastened immediately on the pan of pork and beans that she had left on the stove. "Can I have some of that?"

Surprised, Rebecca answered, "Sure, but it's cold. I can heat it up—"

"Nah, it's okay." He took the spoon she handed him and scraped the contents of the pan into a bowl. Standing in front of the stove, he ate hungrily while Rebecca talked.

"This is going to sound pretty bizarre," she began, "but a man named Mr. Underwood kidnapped me and his little boy—I was baby-sitting for Ethan, the little boy—and brought us up here last night."

The boy nodded. "I saw the car lights—that's when I went up in the attic." He seemed totally unsurprised by her statement about being kidnapped—or maybe he didn't believe her but was just going along with her story. Rebecca couldn't do anything but continue.

"So, anyway, Mr. Underwood went somewhere in the car a while ago, but he was mad because I went outside this morning when he told me not to, so he nailed all the windows shut and locked the door from the outside, and Ethan and I can't get out."

The boy looked skeptical. Setting down his empty bowl, he looked at the window and seemed to notice the boards across it for the first time.

"See, I'm not lying to you—what's your name, anyway?"

He paused for a moment. Then— "Bones," he told her. "You can call me Bones."

It's a good name for someone as skinny as he is, Rebecca thought. "Okay, Bones, and I'm Rebecca," she said. "Anyhow, I don't know what Mr. Underwood is planning to do. Maybe he's trying to get Ethan's mom to pay a ransom for him, or maybe he just wants to scare her, or— oh, I don't know." She didn't add the thought that came next—or maybe he's planning to kill us. But she could see from the considering look in Bones's eyes that he'd come up with that possibility on his own.

Rebecca rushed on. "But it doesn't matter what he's planning to do. The point is, I've got to get out of here with Ethan. And now that you're here, you can help us escape."

Bones shook his head slightly. "I got to get out of here my own self," he told her. "I saw the car go down the hill and I thought you all was gone—didn't know nobody was still in the house. But if the windows can't open and the door be locked from outside—you got to find another key somewhere."

Rebecca stared at him. Of course! Why hadn't she thought of that? If there was another key to the dead bolt on the front door, she could open it whenever she liked.

The late-afternoon light had grown steadily dimmer as they talked. Suddenly there was a brilliant flash, as if from a car's headlights, that reflected off the snow outside the window. "He's coming back!" Rebecca gasped. "You better hide!"

Swiftly and silently Bones moved into the bathroom. Rebecca watched as he stepped onto the toilet seat and reached up to open the trapdoor. Now she could hear the crunching noise of the chains on Mr. Underwood's tires as the car came up the drive. "He's here," she whispered to Bones. "But he'll probably go out again tomorrow." She hoped fervently that her words would come true. "Wait until you see him leave, and then you can help us get away."

The boy looked at her with an expression she couldn't decipher. He didn't say anything and after a moment Rebecca backed out of the little bathroom, closing the door as she went.

While she waited for the slam of Mr. Underwood's car door and for him to turn the key in the lock, her heart beat fast with excitement and hope. How amazing that Bones had been hiding in the attic! She wondered how long he'd been there. And wasn't it lucky that he'd picked this cabin to hide in! Surely between the two of them they could figure out a way to escape. Without thinking what she was doing, Rebecca crossed her fingers in the childhood charm to make wishes come true. If only he could keep from making any noise that would reveal his presence to Mr. Underwood! As the cabin door opened, Rebecca put both hands, with fingers crossed, behind her back.

His arms laden with two large bags, Mr. Underwood shoved the door closed and went into the kitchen. He had apparently decided not to speak to Rebecca unless it was absolutely necessary. In silence he unloaded groceries from a shopping bag—milk, juice, canned soup and SpaghettiOs, bread, peanut butter and jelly, a box of Ritz crackers, and some apples.

From the other bag the man now took several things he'd obviously bought for Ethan. There was a box of crayons and a coloring book, as well as a pad of plain white paper. Among the various other items, what caught Rebecca's eye were a few tapes of children's stories. She was puzzled—how could Ethan play them? Then she saw that

Mr. Underwood had opened the back of a small tape recorder and was putting in new batteries.

"Becca?" The wavering little voice told her that Ethan had awakened from his nap. As she went to get him up, she wasn't sure how she felt about Mr. Underwood's shopping trip. On the one hand, it would be nice for Ethan to have something to play with besides kindling from the fireplace. But on the other hand, gathering all this stuff seemed to indicate that Mr. Underwood planned a long stay at the cabin. Squaring her shoulders, Rebecca thought, I don't care what he's got in mind. We're going to get away from here, and he's not going to stop us!

Afternoon dragged into evening and Rebecca thought time had never passed so slowly. She felt jumpy and lethargic at the same time, and so tired of the inside of the little cabin that she thought she could scream. It was a big help, she had to admit, to have some things for Ethan to play with. He spent a long time coloring in one of the books and then playing a complicated pretend game with the plastic trolls Mr. Underwood had bought. She hadn't seen these colorful little figures for several years—they must have been stashed in the back of whatever toy shop Ethan's father had stopped in—but Ethan was delighted with them.

Mr. Underwood spent most of the time sitting on the couch and staring into the fire. Occasionally Rebecca could hear him muttering to himself, but she couldn't make out the words. She and

Ethan had a supper of SpaghettiOs and apples, and then he listened to some of the story tapes his father had brought. Mr. Underwood still hardly spoke to Ethan at all. Rebecca felt as if she was the interpreter or go-between for two people who couldn't communicate directly with one another.

With nothing to read and no TV to watch, she found the same thoughts going round and round in her brain like mice on a treadmill. What was happening in the world outside—the real world, as she couldn't help calling it to herself? Did anyone know what had happened to her and Ethan, or did it seem they had vanished without a trace? Did Ethan's mother, or the police, suspect that Mr. Underwood was involved? Did they even know it was a kidnapping? And what could she do to help people find them, or to organize their escape?

Every time she heard a sound—a burning log shifting in the fireplace, a click from Ethan's tape recorder—she jumped, terrified that Mr. Underwood would discover Bones's hiding place. She had to stop herself from looking up at the ceiling, and she was grateful when at last Ethan's eyelids began to droop.

The little boy wanted to sleep in her bed again that night, and Rebecca agreed—after all, if being next to her gave him some comfort, why not? As she helped him wash his face, Rebecca wondered what he thought about their situation. He asked no questions, almost as if he was afraid to know what was going on. I don't blame him, Rebecca thought, there's nothing good to know. But she worried about the child, whose normal outgoing manner and ready laughter seemed to have been quenched completely. He was too quiet, too reluctant to draw attention to himself. She almost wished he would cry or throw a tantrum, just to prove that he was still a regular little kid.

She tucked Ethan into bed, and soon afterward she crawled in beside him—there certainly was no reason to stay up in the living room with Mr. Underwood. But she wasn't ready for sleep. Lying in the narrow bunk, she let her mind wander. Soon images of her friends at Porterville High School crowded into her mental movie screen.

Dani, of course, was the person she thought of first. Her friend's animated face, her almond eyes nearly hidden by the shaggy black bangs, swam before her mind's eye, and Rebecca could feel Dani's concern and worry. *Where are you, Rebecca?* The voice was almost real, and Rebecca had to stop herself from answering aloud, *Oh, Dani, I'm trapped and I need help!*

Abruptly Rebecca rubbed her hand across her eyes. *Don't start feeling sorry for yourself—that will definitely not help the situation.* With an effort she dragged her thoughts back to Porterville, but the face that appeared in her mind's eye now was Andy Hollister's. Gorgeous as ever, with that smooth dark hair falling across his forehead, he seemed to gaze at her with a mocking smile twitching the corners of his mouth. "Oh, Rebecca," she imagined him saying with a sorrowful shake of his good-looking head, "you're always rushing into things. Nobody but you could end up kidnapped and snowbound in the Adirondacks! You need to learn to be a little more laid-back—more cool."

Angrily Rebecca shook her head, and then stopped, fearful that she would wake Ethan. But the little boy just sighed in his sleep and snuggled closer to her, while Rebecca thought, Boy, that's just typical of Andy Hollister the third! That's exactly what he would say. Totally unhelpful, totally unsympathetic, just worried about keeping his own image perfect in case a talent scout from a modeling agency in New York City should happen by.

Calming down a bit, she thought, Oh, well, he can't help what he is—a spoiled brat who doesn't have any understanding of real people. I don't know why I ever went out with him.

But of course she did know. He was really good-looking—the classic tall, dark, and handsome type—and he was also smart, rich, and funny. Rebecca had been flattered when he'd asked her out. She'd enjoyed being seen with a popular guy like Andy. If she was honest with herself, she had to admit she'd enjoyed the envy of other girls. And it had taken her a long time to recognize the nasty undertone to his humorous comments. Actually, she thought, I didn't let myself see how mean Andy is until after he broke up with me, so I can't take much credit for it. Face it, Rebecca, you felt humiliated to be dropped by Mr. Cool out of the blue like that—but do you really miss him? No, she answered herself, I don't want to get back together with him. I don't even really like him much. But I don't want him to think I'm moping around after him, hoping he'll change his mind.

Suddenly the absurdity of her thoughts struck her. Andy Hollister—in fact, everyone and everything in Porterville—was totally irrelevant right now. Rebecca shuddered as she thought, You and Ethan could be dead tomorrow. How can you waste time worrying about people you may never see again? A cold wave of fear washed over her, and she burrowed under the blankets, wrapping her arm tight around Ethan's small body. It was up to her to find a way to escape, and she was more determined than ever to do it.

CHAPTER ELEVEN

In the morning Rebecca was tired. She hadn't slept well, awakening countless times to turn over cautiously, afraid she'd wake Ethan but unable to find a comfortable position. She had a confused memory of a dream in which she'd been on vacation with her mom and dad and the three of them had been walking along a stream toward a waterfall. The dream images of her parents made her realize how much she longed to be home. But she couldn't let herself think about home and family, or she'd get too sad. She felt she had to keep all those emotions out of her mind and just deal with what was happening to her in this snowbound cabin.

Now the morning light streamed in through the small window of the bedroom. Rebecca got up and, with a grimace of disgust, pulled on her jeans and sweater again. If I ever get out of this place, I'm going to burn these clothes, she thought.

Ethan was ready to get up, too, and when he was dressed they went out to the kitchen and had bread spread with peanut butter for breakfast. Mr. Underwood had been building a fire and then had gone outside. When he returned, he carried an armful of logs over to the fireplace and dropped them into the basket on the hearth.

With the little tape recorder in his hand, Ethan's father sat down at the table where Ethan was chewing the last sticky bite of bread. He stared at his son and then at Rebecca. Her skin crawled as she waited to find out what was coming next.

At last he spoke in that expressionless voice he seemed to use whenever he talked to Rebecca. "I'm going to make a telephone call today to Ethan's mother," he said. "I want you to make a tape that I will play for her over the phone. Just say that you're well and unharmed, and then Ethan can say the same thing."

Before he had finished talking, Rebecca's mind was racing. This was her chance to communicate with the outside world and let Mrs. Underwood know what had happened to her and Ethan! Furiously she tried to think of clues she could drop into whatever she said. People in books and TV mysteries always seemed able to think of clever ways to disguise information and pass it on to their rescuers. But her brain was refusing to come up with anything helpful.

Could she mention the snow or the woods or the cabin on the hilltop? With dismay Rebecca realized that she didn't actually know where they were. She hadn't even seen which exit Mr. Underwood had taken when he got off the Thruway. But at least she knew they had gone north on the Thruway for more than three hours. If she could just get that fact onto the tape, it had to help people find her and Ethan.

Mr. Underwood was watching her closely, and now his lips curved in a mocking smile. "Whatever you're planning, Miss Harper, don't bother," he said evenly. "Remember, if I don't like what you say on the tape, you can simply be erased."

She flinched at his choice of words and he smiled again. Pushing down the record button, he said, "Testing, testing," into the tiny microphone and then rewound the tape and played back his words. Satisfied that the machine was working, he reached across the table and handed the microphone to Rebecca.

"When I tell you to, you can start talking. But don't say much—just tell my former wife that you are safe and that Ethan is with you. And tell her that today is Thursday. But, Miss Harper—" He fixed her with a cold stare. "Don't mention my name or where you are. Do you understand?"

Rebecca stared back at him, unwilling to let him see how defeated she felt. She wasn't going to be able to pass on any secret messages or to tell Mrs. Underwood anything more than the man wanted her to say. At last she nodded, and he pushed the record button and gestured for her to begin.

"Hi, Mrs. Underwood, this is Rebecca." Instinctively she paused, as if waiting for a reply, but then she realized that this wasn't a telephone call. She went on slowly, "Ethan is with me and he's fine—we're both fine." There didn't seem to be anything else to say. Rebecca started to put the microphone down, and then quickly added, "Oh, yeah, today is Thursday."

Mr. Underwood shut off the recorder and nodded approvingly. Then he turned to his son. "Okay, Ethan, it's your turn. When I tell you to, I want you to say hello to your mother."

The little boy's brown eyes filled with tears, and Rebecca felt a wave of anger wash over her. How could Ethan's own father do this to the child? She leaned over and picked Ethan up, taking him on her lap and cuddling him against her. "Shh, Ethan, sweetie, it's okay, don't worry." Her voice and her arms holding him tight seemed to reassure him.

Rebecca looked across at Mr. Underwood. Surely he wouldn't force his son to go on, now that he could see how much it upset Ethan to be reminded that his mother wasn't here. But the man sat holding the microphone, his face showing no sign of compassion, and Rebecca knew he wasn't going to give up.

She whispered to Ethan, "It's a pretend game, Ethan. Just say 'Hi, Mommy' like you were talking to her on the phone at her work. Okay? Can you do that?"

After a moment the child nodded his head. Rebecca held the microphone and Ethan said hesitantly, "Hi, Mommy. I want to go home."

The catch in his sad little voice tore at her heart and Rebecca wanted to scream at their kidnapper. Hadn't he punished everybody enough? Couldn't he see that his child needed to go home? But she held in her rage, knowing that angry shouting would scare Ethan even more, and fearful of what Mr. Underwood's reaction might be.

She sat, still holding Ethan close, and watched as Mr. Underwood put on his parka and prepared to leave the cabin. Slipping the tape recorder into his pocket, he told her, "I will lock the door again from the outside, so you needn't trouble yourself to try to get out." Just as she had the day before, she listened to the clicks as he bolted the door and to the roar of the car's engine starting up.

Five minutes later Ethan wanted to get down from her lap and play with his little trolls. Rebecca marveled at his ability to forget about feeling unhappy and wanting to go home. She almost envied the way he could focus on whatever was going on here and now.

As she watched Ethan set up a pretend school for his trolls, she heard a muffled sound from the bathroom. Soon the door opened and Bones cautiously poked his head out. Rebecca gestured toward the kitchen, and he silently disappeared around the corner. She watched Ethan for another few moments and then left him absorbed in his game while she joined Bones in the kitchen.

He was eating a slice of bread from the bag on the counter, and holding another slice in his other hand. He must be starving, Rebecca realized. But she couldn't give him much of the food Mr. Underwood had brought yesterday—the man would notice if it was all gone. Then she had a flash of inspiration—he could eat some of the canned pork and beans from the cupboard. Since Mr. Underwood hadn't bought it, he probably didn't know exactly how many cans were there and wouldn't know if one was missing. Quickly explaining this in a low voice, she opened a can and dumped it into a pan.

Turning on the stove, she said, "What are you doing here, anyway?"

Bones raised his eyes from the food in the pan and gazed consideringly at Rebecca. Then he said flatly, "I ran away. From St. Ignatius." Seeing her frown of puzzlement, he went on, "It's a school for kids that mess up and get in trouble. I was in a foster home in Newburgh, and then they sent me up here. But now—" He shook his head. "I ain't never going back there, and not to Newburgh either. Couldn't *pay* me to go back to them folks."

The food was bubbling slightly in the pan, and as Rebecca ladled it into a bowl for Bones, she asked, "So where will you go?"

"Canada," he answered, blowing on the beans to cool them. "I hear it's a pretty cool place—ain't so much prejudice as we got here in the ol' U.S. of A. I'll get me a job and . . ." He smiled at her for the first time. "Least I won't be in St. Ignatius. Can't be worse than that."

"But what about your family?" Rebecca found it impossible to imagine herself setting off for Canada on her own. Was Bones serious or was he putting her on?

"Don't have one," he told her, the flat tone back in his voice. "They're all dead or disappeared long ago. I been in foster care since I was eight. And that's been eight years too long."

Rebecca stood up and went to the doorway. She didn't know what to say. Spending half of one's life with foster families sounded so awful. But she wasn't sure Bones needed or wanted sympathy from her. She looked into the living room. Ethan was still sitting on the floor in front of the couch, his trolls now living in a house made of sticks of firewood. He seemed content by himself, so she retreated quietly into the kitchen.

Bones placed his empty bowl in the sink. He looked at the window and then at Rebecca. "He lock you in again?"

"Yes. But I wanted to ask you, isn't there some way to get out from the attic?"

Shaking his head doubtfully, Bones replied, "There's a little bitty window. But even if you could squeeze through it, there's nothing to hold on to to climb down. I might be able to get out that way, but for you and the kid—uh-uh."

"Well, if you can get out, you can find someplace where there's a phone and call my parents or the police and tell them where we are." The idea that it might actually be possible to escape was so exciting, Rebecca had to remind herself to keep her voice down.

But Bones shook his head, this time with emphasis. "When I get out of here, I ain't going noplace to make no phone calls. Somebody see me and send me back to St. Ignatius. I mean, ain't so many people look like me out here in the backwoods. I be as obvious as a ant in a sugar bowl." He smiled, a sarcastic twist of his lips that didn't reach his eyes.

"Oh, Bones, you've got to! It's just a phone call, but we've got to get out of here. I didn't tell you yet, but he made us talk on a tape before he left—he said he was going to play it on the phone for Ethan's mother. It sounds like he's planning to hold us, or at least Ethan, for ransom. But it could take days and days for that to happen, and we've got to get out of here!" Embarrassed by the desperation in her voice, Rebecca fell silent.

Bones looked at her as if considering her situation for the first time. "Yeah," he said at last, "and besides, once he gets that ransom . . ." He didn't finish the sentence, but Rebecca could complete it for him: *Once he gets that ransom, he won't need to keep you alive anymore.*

"Becca?"

Oh, no, Rebecca thought, I forgot all about Ethan. I hope he didn't hear what I was saying. The child sidled over to her and clutched her leg, staring at Bones in confusion. "Becca, who's that?" he asked softly.

Reaching down to ruffle Ethan's hair, Rebecca wondered frantically what she could say to explain

Bones's presence. It was vitally important to keep Mr. Underwood from suspecting the existence of another person in the cabin. How could she make sure Ethan didn't say anything?

While Bones stood immobile, his face a mask of dismay, Rebecca said carefully, "He's my secret friend, Ethan. Now you know the secret, too. But we have to keep it secret from your dad, or else my friend can't come and talk to me anymore. Okay? Can you remember not to tell your dad about him?"

Ethan looked up at her and nodded. "Yeah, Becca, I can keep a secret."

"Good!" She took the little boy's hand and turned to leave the kitchen. "Let's go in here and you show me what your trolls have been doing."

The child went with her willingly, though he glanced back once at Bones's motionless form. When they sat down on the floor in front of the couch, Rebecca made sure that Ethan's back was to the bathroom door. She talked about the trolls for a few moments, and then said, "Ethan, these trolls are kind of magic, aren't they? They can do stuff that regular people can't do."

Ethan nodded seriously, and Rebecca continued, "Well, my secret friend is magic, too. He can just appear and disappear whenever he wants, sort of like the magic people in fairy tales."

"Like the fairy godmother?" Ethan asked.

"Yes, exactly," she answered, grateful that he knew the story of "Cinderella." She hoped it would make it easier for him to believe in a "magic" Bones. That way, even if he talked about Bones when his father was around, it would sound as if he were talking about an imaginary person.

"Yes, just like the fairy godmother," she went on, raising her voice slightly. "You know how she just appears and disappears and you don't know where she came from or where she went?" Come on, Bones, she thought, take the hint and "disappear" into the attic while Ethan isn't looking. She couldn't risk having Ethan see where the boy went. It would be too hard for him not to talk about the trapdoor in front of his father.

"Yeah, and Tinkerbell does that, too!" Ethan was getting right into the spirit of the conversation.

"That's right, she does." Rebecca saw Bones peer cautiously into the living room and then slip from kitchen to bathroom door without a sound. She kept talking. "Isn't it amazing how they can do that? Just suddenly pop into somewhere, and then later on, pop! They're gone. Did you ever think you'd see a magic man like that?"

Ethan shook his head solemnly. Then he twisted around to look toward the kitchen. "Is your secret friend still there?"

"I don't know," she answered. "Let's go and see."

As they walked into the kitchen, Rebecca heard a soft scraping noise. Inwardly she sighed with relief—Bones was back up in the attic.

Ethan was standing in the doorway. "He's not here," he told Rebecca. "Will he come back?"

"I don't know," she said. "You never can tell about magic people."

CHAPTER TWELVE

Sergeant Van Kerelin ran his hand over his short blond hair and sighed. This was awful. Talking to a woman whose child had been kidnapped was about the hardest thing he'd ever done in his fifteen years on the Porterville police force. And by now the police were definitely going on the assumption that it was a kidnapping.

Sipping coffee at Marian Underwood's kitchen table, he looked across at her drawn face. She must be exhausted, he thought sympathetically. It was no wonder. If one of his own kids had vanished into thin air the way little Ethan had, he knew he and his wife wouldn't be able to sleep a wink until the child was found.

"So, anyway, Mrs. Underwood, we've been in touch with the local police up in New Hampshire, and according to them, Mr. Underwood hasn't been to work for almost two weeks. He told them he had to go out of town on family business, and they aren't expecting him back until the end of next week at the earliest. And he told his landlady the same thing." Van Kerelin paused, and then went on, "He didn't leave anyone an address where they could reach him. So we need to know, does he have family somewhere that you know of, that he might be visiting?"

Marian shook her head drearily. "My ex-husband doesn't have any family. He was an only child, and both his parents died soon after he finished college."

"Okay, but what about other family members?" Van persisted. "Grandparents still alive, or cousins, aunts and uncles?"

"No," Marian answered, "his grandparents are all dead. And I never heard of any cousins—I don't think he has any. But wait a minute. There was an aunt somewhere in Ohio, I think her name is Evelyn. But he never saw her—just exchanged cards at Christmas, you know the kind of thing."

"You never know, maybe he went to visit her," Van said, opening his notebook. "Is her last name Underwood, too? And do you remember what town in Ohio she lives in?"

"Yes," Marian told him, "I think her name is Underwood—she's Harley's father's sister. But as for the town, I have no idea. Some small town in central Ohio, that's all I can remember."

"Okay, let me call the station," Van said. He picked up the phone and soon was telling someone to get the Ohio state cops to look for an Evelyn Underwood, because it was just possible her nephew Harley Underwood was visiting her, and if he was, the Porterville police wanted to talk to him.

When he hung up, Marian said abruptly, "If he's there, visiting his aunt in Ohio, where does that get us?"

"Well, if he's there and he doesn't have Ethan with him, then we'll know it isn't him who kidnapped your little boy," Van told her gently.

"But it has to be him," Marian burst out. "There's no one else who could do such a horrible thing to Ethan, and to me. He hates me, he thinks I took his baby away from him."

Van nodded. "I think you're probably right, but we have to check everything out, just in case. And until we find him, or hear from him, I want you to keep thinking of possible places where he might have gone with Ethan. Places he talked about, places he went on vacations, places he always wanted to visit—anything you can think of that might give us a lead to follow."

Marian stared at him, her eyes filled with tears. "I told you, he never talked about anyplace except New Hampshire, he had this idea that he'd like to live in the mountains away from cities and crowds of people, he doesn't like crowds. But you already know that, and if he's not there where he lives—"

"We're going to keep checking," Van said soothingly. "Don't worry, we're going to find Ethan." And I hope that's true, he thought.

"You have to!" Marian wailed. "My poor baby! And poor Rebecca, too!" She put her head down on the table and sobbed.

A few blocks away Bob and Ellen Harper sat at their own kitchen table. Kathy Delarra sat with them. Although her son Joe hadn't been a Porterville cop very long, he was part of the active investigation. Kathy called him every night either at the station or at his small apartment, and she knew there was no good news. Her heart ached for her friends Bob and Ellen, and she stopped by as often as she could to lend some quiet support and comfort.

Kathy poured some tea into Ellen's cup and then put her hand on her friend's arm. "Ellen, dear, do you think you could try to sleep a little?"

Rebecca's mother shook her head. "No, I'd just lie there tossing and turning, wondering where Rebecca and little Ethan are." She stopped and then said despairingly, "It's the not knowing that's so hard! Not knowing where they are, and what happened—why they disappeared like that."

Kathy stroked her friend's arm. "I know, it's just awful. But I'm sure you'll hear something soon. You've got to."

Ellen gave her a strained smile and then sipped her tea. Bob Harper said quietly, "What makes it so difficult to understand is that we don't even know for sure if this is a kidnapping, and if so, if it was Ethan who was kidnapped and Rebecca just got taken along with him, or if it was Rebecca they were after and somehow Ethan was caught up in whatever was going on."

Kathy nodded quietly. It was heartbreaking to watch her friends go through this dreadful ordeal, and trying to be so brave about it. Thank goodness her own children were grown up and on their own now—although you never stopped worrying about your kids, no matter how old they were.

Ellen was saying, "I've thought and thought about it, and I can't think of anyone who would have done this to Rebecca. I mean, kidnapped her—and it seems as if they've pretty much ruled out everything else by now, like a hit-and-run accident or whatever. But we don't have any money, so it couldn't be anything like that. And I just can't imagine anyone who dislikes us, or dislikes Rebecca, enough to do this terrible thing."

"No," her husband agreed, "and besides, the police have talked to her friends from school, and to Andy, that guy she used to go out with. And they're sure none of the kids knows anything at all. But of course, you know all this, Kathy, you must hear about it from Joe."

Kathy nodded. "I do hear a few things, of course, Joe knows I'm so concerned about Rebecca and about you two. He said they had talked with Dani, Rebecca's friend."

Rebecca's mother sighed. "Yes, and apparently she told the police that Rebecca had gotten some peculiar phone calls when she was at Mrs. Underwood's house—you know, calls where no one says anything when you pick up." Her eyes filled with tears. "I wish she had told us about them. I can't help feeling that there must be some clue that we've all missed, some *reason* for this to have happened. I can't stand the idea that it's completely senseless, because I feel as if that means there was no rhyme or reason for it to have happened. Oh, I'm just so frustrated, I want to scream and shout and throw things."

Her husband smiled sadly. "Go ahead and scream, honey, I know just how you feel." He clenched his hands into tight fists. "It's terrible to know there's nothing you can do, no one you can grab hold of and shake until they tell you where Rebecca and Ethan are and what's happening to them." He looked at his hands and slowly opened his fists. "We're all just sitting here, waiting for the phone to ring."

CHAPTER THIRTEEN

Mr. Underwood was gone for a long time—so long that Rebecca had begun to spin a hopeful fantasy in which he had been picked up by the police in some nearby town, perhaps while he was making his phone call to Ethan's mother, and any minute their police cars would come up the long curving drive to rescue her and Ethan. But when she did at last hear a car, disappointment hit her in a great wave. It was Mr. Underwood.

He came inside and looked over to where Rebecca and Ethan were drawing pictures of animals. Ethan was giggling over the idea of a purple rabbit with green polka dots and he barely looked up when his father arrived. Mr. Underwood carried a small bag that must contain groceries into the kitchen.

In a few minutes he came out again and walked

over to the table. He stood watching Rebecca and Ethan without saying a word, and Rebecca's palms began to tingle with nervousness. This was the moment she had been dreading. What if Ethan said something to his father about Bones, or asked a question that revealed Bones's presence in the cabin? Rebecca could only hope that the child wouldn't say anything, or if he did, that she could make it sound like a reference to a fairy tale.

Ethan glanced up quickly at his father and then returned his attention to his drawing, picking up a black crayon and starting to color over a small turquoise bird. He pressed so hard on the crayon that it broke in two.

"Becca, look, my crayon broke." He held it out to her.

"Oh, well, don't worry about it. I'll just peel off some of the paper and you can use whichever piece you want." She handed the two sections of crayon back to him. "But how come you're covering up everything with black? I can't see your bird anymore."

The little boy nodded soberly. "It was bad, and I didn't want it."

His statement startled Rebecca. After a moment she said, "I didn't think it was bad." She watched as he continued to scribble over his drawing, his face set in a frown of concentration.

Mr. Underwood moved away from the table, still without a word, and Rebecca realized that she didn't have to worry about Ethan telling him

about Bones. The boy almost never spoke directly
to his father. It was as if he was trying to pretend
the man didn't exist. Still, Rebecca knew that Mr.
Underwood listened to every word she and Ethan
exchanged. She'd just have to be super-careful, at
least until Bones managed to find a way to get
out of the cabin and she persuaded him to find a
telephone and call the police.

Darkness came early, filling the cabin with deep
gloomy shadows. Rebecca waited while Mr. Underwood lit the candles and then she went into the
kitchen to make supper for Ethan and herself. It
was somehow taken for granted that she would
prepare food for the two of them, and not for
Mr. Underwood. Rebecca repressed a shudder.
She wouldn't find it easy to cook for this horrible
person.

As she was stirring the food in the pan (canned
ravioli this time), Mr. Underwood walked behind
her to the counter and poured himself a glass of
apple juice. He frowned as he set the jar down.
"What's happened to the juice? This bottle was
full this morning."

Rebecca shrugged as nonchalantly as she could,
but her stomach was tying itself in knots. Bones
had drunk at least two big glasses of the juice!
She couldn't exactly blame him—there was no
water up in the attic, she felt sure. Aloud she
said, "We drank it. The water doesn't taste very
good." Inwardly she prayed, Just let him believe
me.

Mr. Underwood muttered something that she

didn't catch and then, mercifully, walked out of the kitchen. Quickly Rebecca called Ethan to come to the table, hoping the man would stay at the other end of the main room.

After they had finished, Rebecca and Ethan sat in front of the fire. In spite of having spent the entire day cooped up in the cabin, Ethan seemed tired, and he was content to listen to one of his stories on the tape recorder Mr. Underwood had brought back with him. When it was over, he said to Rebecca, "Now you tell me a story, Becca. Tell a story about the magic man."

Her heart raced furiously while for a moment her mind went completely blank. How could she make up a story that wouldn't sound too real? And she'd have to think up a name for the "magic man"—she couldn't very well call him Bones. Like the miller's daughter in the fairy tale, she needed a name—and then it hit her. Of course, the name she needed was Rumpelstiltskin.

"I know a good story about a magic man, Ethan. Let me just think how it starts." After a moment she began, telling about the miller who bragged that his daughter could spin straw into gold and the little magic man who appeared out of nowhere to help her perform this impossible task. When she got to the part where the queen tries to guess the magic man's name, she couldn't remember the names in her old book. But it didn't much matter, so she made up the silliest ones she could.

" 'Is your name Bundlebug? Cricklecrack? Dingledoggie?' " Rebecca was pleased to see

Ethan smiling delightedly at these absurd names, and she asked him what names he would guess if he were the queen.

"Googlegoggle," he said tentatively, and then went on, "How about Hungerbunger? Or Paggie-waggie?" Giggling, he added several more before she went on with the story.

When she got near the end, she lowered her voice almost to a whisper. "And then the queen said, 'Is your name' "—Rebecca paused dramatically—" 'Rumpelstiltskin?' " She wound up the tale, and Ethan snuggled against her.

"Rumpelstiltskin," he said slowly, savoring the word. "That was a good story, Becca."

Hugging him hard, Rebecca told him, "I'm glad you liked it."

"Can I hear it again?" he asked hopefully.

"When you're in bed and all ready for sleep, I'll tell it to you again," she promised. To herself she thought, It's lucky I could remember that whole story—it took his mind off Bones, at least for now.

But when he was sound asleep and she had gone to bed herself, stretching out next to him under the layers of blankets, Rebecca couldn't make herself relax. She kept listening for the slightest noise over her head. Was Bones still up there, or had he figured out how to get out of the small window he'd told her about? Was he already on his way to Canada, trudging through the snowy woods? If he was, would he stop somewhere and call the police—he didn't know her last name, or Ethan's, so he couldn't very well call their homes. But he seemed like a nice enough person. In spite of his fear of being caught himself, surely he wouldn't just go off and leave them trapped without doing something to help them.

Someone was talking out in the living room! Had somebody else arrived at the cabin? She wasn't sure whether she should be elated or scared, but Rebecca knew she had to find out who Mr. Underwood was talking to.

Edging cautiously out from under the blankets, she hurriedly pulled on her clothes and then crept to the door of the little bedroom. The talking was still going on, but she couldn't distinguish any words.

Slowly and carefully, exerting pressure so the hinges wouldn't squeal, Rebecca opened the door about an inch and peered out into the living room. Against the flickering glow from the fireplace she could see the shadowy shape of Mr. Underwood sitting on the couch, his back to her. But there was no one else, at least not in her field of vision. Then she realized that he was talking into the little microphone of the tape recorder. Was he making a new tape to play on the phone tomorrow for Ethan's mother? She had to know what he was saying.

Opening the door a bit wider, she focused all her attention on the voice that rose and fell in the quiet room. "I have my son now, and I won't let anybody take him away again, I have waited too long and been through too much. . . . You know what I'm talking about, Marian, don't pretend you don't. . . . I have worked things though in my mind, and I will not need quite as much money as we discussed before, only approximately half that much if things go the way I plan. . . . But I need firm assurances—*firm* assurances—that there will be no police, no army or navy or marines set on my trail. Do you understand, *no one* is to follow me or harass me in any way, I have had enough harassment to last several lifetimes, and I will not be responsible for the consequences if this order is disobeyed."

He stopped talking, and Rebecca found she was trembling violently. The bedroom was cold, but that wasn't the reason she was shaking from head to foot. It was Mr. Underwood. He sounded so weird. She couldn't follow everything he was saying, but it seemed that he planned to keep Ethan with him instead of returning him to his mother, and he also wanted some money.

The voice in the other room began again, and she tried to pick up what he was saying.

"Consequences—every action has its consequence, yours as well as mine, and the matter is in your hands now to make sure that the consequences are the correct and appropriate ones. . . . How can you know the consequences, you ask? My response: Use whatever brains you have left in that head, whatever intelligence has not been crowded out by evil thoughts translated into evil deeds. . . . I repeat, the consequences are on your head now, in your hands, at your feet. . . .

My son is a personable child, but his upbringing has made him fearful, has turned him against me, and all this will take time to work out, and I must have time. . . . If I am not given enough time, if my orders are not obeyed, I will be forced to adopt a new plan, and one that will not include my son or the young woman who is caring for him, they are expendable, they are not necessary elements of the master plan. . . . Have I made myself clear? This is not to be construed as a threat, merely as a statement of fact, I do not deal in threats but in simple factual realities, I am not like other people. . . ."

His words trailed off again, and Rebecca stood frozen in terror. The man sounded completely crazy, but at the same time there were threads running through his monologue. And if she understood those underlying threads correctly, he intended to get rid of both her and Ethan if his "orders" weren't carried out the way he wanted.

Even if his orders were obeyed, which she gathered meant he would get some amount of money and a promise that the police wouldn't try to catch him, he would take Ethan away with him somewhere—but what would he do with her?

Expendable—that was the word he had used. Swallowing hard, Rebecca forced her mind to admit what that really meant: Mr. Underwood would kill her.

Moving slowly and with great effort, as if she were underwater, Rebecca closed the bedroom door and crawled back into the bed where Ethan slept.

He turned restlessly and she put her hand on his shoulder to quiet him. Tears leaked slowly from her eyes and made a wet spot on the pillow as she thought in hopeless despair, If we don't get out of here, we could both be dead.

CHAPTER FOURTEEN

The next morning Rebecca woke up and for a moment couldn't remember where she was. Puzzled and disoriented, she gazed upward at the slats of the upper bunk over her head and then turned to look at the other set of bunk beds across the room. Recognition descended on her then, a heavy weight that made her close her eyes and wish that she could retreat once more into sleep.

But it didn't work, and soon she sighed and pulled herself out of bed, careful not to wake the still-sleeping child next to her. As she dressed she thought, It's Friday morning. This is our third day in this place. I wonder what Mom and Dad are doing.

With a sense of surprise Rebecca realized that she hadn't thought much about home since she'd arrived at the cabin. It wasn't that she didn't have time to think about it—there was nothing *but* time while she was locked up with no way of escape. And it certainly wasn't that she didn't miss her family. She longed for home, for her parents, for her friends, with a yearning so fierce she felt it might consume her if she let it.

But she couldn't afford to think about how much she wanted to be home. She had to concentrate every minute on what was happening right here. She had to protect herself and Ethan from the man she now privately considered very disturbed, and she had to be on the alert for any possible chance of escape. There would be time enough to think about home if she ever got back there. *When* I get back there, she corrected herself, determined not to give way to pessimism.

Mr. Underwood stood up from the hearth as Rebecca emerged from the bedroom, brushing ashes from his hands. Rebecca couldn't help shuddering slightly, remembering the strange and frightening rambling she had overheard the night before. Thinking of what he had said made her bold, or maybe desperate.

"Mr. Underwood, please won't you let Ethan and me leave here today? I know my parents must be so worried about me." She wasn't sure whether to add anything about Ethan's mother, but decided against it—Mr. Underwood might get upset.

He looked at her with that slight sarcastic smile she'd seen before and just shook his head.

Now that she'd started, Rebecca had to keep trying. "But why are you doing this? Why are you keeping us here? Oh, please, won't you tell me what's going to happen after you—" She broke off abruptly, dismayed at the terrified note in her voice and at the way she'd almost referred to the plans he had mentioned on the tape.

Sure enough, he glared at her and asked angrily, "After what, Miss Harper?"

Searching for a response, she said weakly, "After you played the tape Ethan and I talked on yesterday."

Still fixing her with a cold stare, he said, "You will learn what I choose to tell you, no more and no less."

Rebecca turned away toward the kitchen. It was hopeless. He wouldn't tell her anything about what was going on, and he obviously wasn't influenced in the slightest by her pleading. She felt defeated— she might as well give up. But then she thought, No, I'm not going to just sit and wait for disaster. I have to try to get Ethan and myself out of here, somehow.

She heard the cabin door close. Moving to the window, she could see Mr. Underwood walking to his car and getting in. But he didn't start it—just sat in the driver's seat, leaning toward the dashboard. Was there something wrong with the car?

Then the answer clicked in her mind. Of course, he must be listening to the radio. He probably wanted to find out if there was any mention of a kidnapping on the news. He'd probably be out there twenty minutes or so—that was the length of time the news stations spent on one cycle of news reports.

Could she make use of this time by herself? It was no use thinking about leaving the cabin, even though she was pretty sure Mr. Underwood hadn't double-locked the door. He would see her as soon as she set foot outside. Then Rebecca's gaze fell on the tape recorder, sitting on the edge of the table.

What if she added a message to the tape the man had made last night? Surely he was planning to play it over the telephone. Maybe she could tell where she and Ethan were, or say something that would give a clue to the people who must be searching for them.

Rebecca picked up the machine and found the record button. But then she set it down again on the table and backed away. It was too much of a risk. Mr. Underwood was likely to listen to the tape either before he made his call or while he was playing it over the phone. Either way, he'd be furious with Rebecca. And he could get back to the cabin before any rescuers could possibly find it. Unconsciously she shook her head. No, she couldn't take the chance that he would do something to hurt her or Ethan if he found out.

She heard Ethan stirring in the bedroom and went to get him up. His face looked flushed and his eyes were a little puffy. Rebecca laid her hand on his forehead the way her own mother had done to her a million times. She wasn't sure how warm or cool it was supposed to feel, but Ethan's skin seemed too warm. Was he coming down with a cold? Or with something worse?

When the little boy burst into angry tears because there was once again no cereal for breakfast, Rebecca felt sure that something was wrong. Even with all the tension of being cooped up here with the father he scarcely knew, away from his mom and his home, Ethan had been so good—almost too good. Maybe I should tell Mr. Underwood that Ethan is sick, Rebecca thought. Maybe that will make him let us go home.

In another part of her mind the warning signs went up. Don't tell him! Who knows what he might do? For sure he'll get mad, and maybe blame you or Ethan himself for his being sick. The fear she had felt last night as she listened to Mr. Underwood's confused and angry words returned in a rush. He had made it clear that if everything didn't go the way he wanted, he would do something drastic—Rebecca made herself admit that what Mr. Underwood had been talking about was killing her and Ethan. She knew she couldn't let him know anything was wrong with his son.

The door slammed and Ethan's father walked into the cabin. Rebecca desperately wanted to ask him what he had heard on the news radio. Did the news people know about the kidnapping, or had it been kept completely quiet? Was anyone looking for her and Ethan? Did the police know what had happened? She didn't know whether it would be better for news of their kidnapping to be broadcast all over the state or if Mr. Underwood was more likely to let them go home if no one except their families knew they were missing. But she hated being so entirely in the dark. It made her feel helpless, like a pawn in someone else's chess game.

Still, one look at Mr. Underwood's expressionless face made Rebecca decide to keep quiet. She'd already annoyed him with her earlier questions. Better not to cause him any more aggravation.

For most of the morning she and Ethan sat in front of the fire and colored in the coloring books. It had begun to snow outside, and the light in the cabin was dim and gray. Ethan listened to a story tape and then demanded a "new" one: "I'm bored of these stories!" he whined. Rebecca soothed him and put her hand again on his forehead. It felt warmer than ever and she tried to think what to do.

Finally she looked in her purse and fished out the Tylenol she used for occasional headaches. In the kitchen she broke one of the tablets and picked out a piece that was about a quarter of the whole thing. Surely that wouldn't be too much for a three-year-old. Looking over her shoulder to make sure Mr. Underwood wasn't watching her, she mashed the medicine with a spoon and then mixed it with a spoonful of the grape jelly. Luckily Ethan wandered in and wanted juice, and she managed to feed him the jelly without any discussion that Mr. Underwood might over-hear. Rebecca wasn't sure exactly why she was convinced that the idea of Ethan having a fever would send his father into a rage, but she couldn't shake the feeling of certainty.

Soon afterward Ethan fell asleep on the floor, a crayon still clutched in his hand. Rebecca gathered him up and took him into the bedroom. She hoped he'd wake up refreshed and feeling better after a nap.

The time dragged so slowly that Rebecca thought she might start screaming or jumping up and down in frustration. Get it together, Rebecca, she told herself, don't annoy the man. She sat for a while and watched the snow, now falling harder than ever. Then, with one of Ethan's crayons, she began to make a list of stories she could tell him: "Cinderella," "Hansel and Gretel," "The Three Little Pigs." So many of the tales she remembered had evil witches or stepmothers or other wicked characters, and she wondered if these stories would be bad for Ethan right now or if it might help him to hear about storybook people in difficult situations.

A little after noon she made herself eat some lunch—more peanut butter on plain bread. She was getting pretty tired of it herself, and she couldn't really blame poor little Ethan for wanting something different to eat. While she ate she watched Mr. Underwood make several trips out to the woodshed behind the cabin. He brought in a lot of logs, tracking in more snow each time, and piled them up next to the fireplace. Perhaps he was afraid so much snow would fall that he wouldn't be able to get out for more wood later on. Or perhaps he was planning to leave the cabin and thought he might be gone a long time.

This last idea was confirmed when he told Rebecca that he was going out to buy food. She had seen him slip the little tape recorder into his jacket pocket, and she figured he was planning to make another phone call to Ethan's mother while he was out. She simply nodded when he said he was leaving, and he didn't bother to tell her that the door would be locked from the outside. It made Rebecca shudder to realize that they had fallen into a routine. How could life with a kidnapper in an isolated cabin become ordinary? Was this what happened to people in prison? Did they begin to accept life in prison as normal? The idea appalled her.

CHAPTER FIFTEEN

As soon as the car had disappeared down the drive, Rebecca ran into the bathroom. To her great relief, the trapdoor was already open and Bones's long legs were dangling through the opening. Rebecca realized that she'd been afraid he had found a way out of the attic and had left without her knowing it.

Looking at Bones as he jumped lightly to the floor, she knew she had to find a way to talk him into making a phone call for help as soon as he got away. He probably wanted to leave as soon as he could—as the snow got deeper it would be harder to walk through. And it would be harder for the police to get to the cabin, she realized. Well, Bones just had to agree to help.

"I'm hungry," he told her matter-of-factly and headed for the kitchen. Rebecca followed him, trying to figure out the best way to persuade him.

Bones took out a can of the inevitable pork and beans—there weren't many left, Rebecca noticed—and emptied it into a pan on the stove. Stirring it, he said, "Soon as I eat, I'm out of here. I was just waiting for the guy to leave so he wouldn't hear me. But now I'm gonna squeeze through that little window up in the attic and drop down." He waved his spoon toward the front of the cabin.

Great! Rebecca thought. I'm sure I can convince him to call the cops and get help for us. But before she opened her mouth, the image of the three of them—Ethan, herself, and Mr. Underwood—trapped in the cabin, maybe snowbound for days, while they waited for something to happen flashed across her mental screen, and she shuddered.

I can't do it, she thought. I can't stay here and wait for someone else to rescue us, and wonder when Mr. Underwood is going to lose it completely. He sounded close to the edge last night, and the least little thing may make him snap. He could decide anytime that Ethan and I are "expendable."

But what else can I do? Gazing at Bones, she thought, If it's possible for him to get out that window, we can, too. And that's what we have to do. The whole reason we're in this awful situation in the first place is because I went along with what Ethan's father wanted me to do and hoped everything would work out okay. I can't do that again.

She was still staring at Bones, and now he said slowly, "I been thinking about you and the kid stuck here with that guy. I'm still not making any phone calls, but I guess I'll help you and the kid get out if you want—it's a long drop down to that little roof thing and you'd never do it by yourself."

"Oh, Bones, thanks!" Surprising both of them, Rebecca flung her arms around his tall frame and hugged him. Then she stepped back, feeling her face redden. She hadn't meant to embarrass herself, or him for that matter. But she'd been so afraid, without letting herself put it into words, that he would refuse to help her and Ethan at all, or that he'd already left, or—she didn't know what. Energy flowed through her as she thought, I don't have to do it all by myself.

Now Bones was eating the barely warmed food out of the pan with a spoon. "Okay," he said, pausing for a moment, "but we got to go right away. I don't have no time to wait around. So you got to make up your mind."

"Yes," Rebecca said, "of course we're coming. I just have to get myself organized." While she spoke she was already gathering up the food that was left in the little kitchen. Not the cans, she thought, too heavy and I'd have to worry about a can opener. But the few remaining pieces of bread could be spread with peanut butter and jelly. She worked quickly, slapping the sandwiches together and stuffing them back into the plastic bread wrapper. The rest of the crackers and the last two apples joined them. Maybe this is stupid, she thought, maybe I'll find a safe place really quickly. But if I don't, I'll need something to eat, and Ethan hasn't even had any lunch.

Leaving the little collection of food on the counter, Rebecca opened the lower cupboard where she had seen the boots and gloves two days ago. She let out her breath in relief—the jumbled heap was still there. Yanking everything out, she saw with dismay that both pairs of boots were made for men with enormous feet. They'd fall right off if she tried to walk in them, especially in the snow. But her own leather boots were useless for trekking through winter woods. Maybe she could— She cast a glance around the kitchen, conscious that Bones had nearly finished the pork and beans and would want to leave soon. What if she stuffed the huge boots with wadded-up paper towels? That should keep them on her feet if she laced them up tight.

The heavy work gloves were made of unlined leather, stiff with years of dirt. But they would fit over her own gloves and add extra warmth. She put them next to the boots. Glancing at Bones, she said, "Do you have any boots up in the attic? If you don't, you should take this other pair if it'll fit you."

Looking surprised, Bones nodded. While he thrust a foot into one of the boots, Rebecca opened up the jacket that had been at the bottom of the pile. It was large and very old, its cotton fabric worn thin at the wrists and elbows. But it would keep her a little warmer and drier if she put it over her own short jacket. Wryly Rebecca thought, I didn't come prepared for a blizzard.

What else should she take? A blanket—Ethan would need something extra to keep him warm. She was trying not to think about the fact that a long walk through the snow was not the best idea for a three-year-old with a fever. They didn't have any choice. But at least she could keep him as warm as possible.

She tiptoed into the bedroom and brought out one of the extra blankets. When she added it to the pile of food, Bones shook his head in disgust. "How you going to carry all that stuff? You don't need it anyway." He shifted impatiently. "Come on, Rebecca, get the kid and let's get out of here. I can't wait no longer. And besides, when that guy comes back, you don't want to be here."

"I know, I know," Rebecca answered, fear clutching at her, "but Ethan is sick and I've got to take some food and something to keep him warm. Maybe I can tie the other stuff up in the blanket, at least for a while, or—" She gazed wildly around the room as if a bag or something would materialize that she could use to carry everything.

"Aw, come on," Bones growled. "There's some old backpack somebody left up in the attic—you can put your stuff in that."

Rebecca smiled thankfully. "Oh, great, that'll be perfect."

"But let's go—now!" Bones unfolded the blanket partway and rolled the various items of food into it, then carried it into the bathroom.

As quickly as she could, Rebecca tore off paper towels, crumpled them, and stuffed them into the toes of the big boots. Pushing her feet in, she added more paper towels, poking them down around her heels with two fingers. Then she laced up the boots, pulling them tight around her ankles. When she tried walking, her feet felt awkward and heavy, but so far the boots were staying on fairly well. She ripped off several more towels and stuffed them into her pockets. Then she went to get Ethan.

Thank goodness she hadn't bothered to undress him earlier—he was still in the now grubby outfit he'd been wearing since the day they were kidnapped. Hurrying him along, she helped him put on his sneakers and jacket. I'll have to carry him, she thought. His feet will be soaked in a minute without boots.

His face was still flushed and it was hard to keep him awake. Driven by the fear that Mr. Underwood would come back before they could get away, Rebecca nevertheless clomped back into the kitchen and put together another spoonful of jelly with mashed Tylenol in it. It was the only way she knew of to try to bring his fever down.

At the last minute Rebecca took another of the folded blankets from the end of the upper bunk. If she had to carry Ethan, maybe she could tie it into some kind of sling across her back. Finally, snatching up her purse, Rebecca saw her leather boots next to the bed and nearly started crying.

They had been so beautiful, and now they looked pathetic, in need of a lot of tender loving care. Angrily she rubbed her hand across her eyes. Forget it, Rebecca, she thought, if the worst that happens is you leave your favorite boots behind, you'll be in good shape.

Shooing Ethan in front of her, she rushed into the bathroom. Above her head, Bones peered down through the trapdoor. Without a word Rebecca handed him the extra blanket and her purse, as well as the big jacket she'd found. Then, moving awkwardly in the big boots, she climbed onto the toilet seat and bent to pick up Ethan. For a moment she thought she had lost her balance and would fall, but she staggered slightly and caught herself. Slowly she lifted the little boy as high as she could, her arms and shoulders burning with the effort. And then Bones's long arms grasped the child and drew him up through the trapdoor.

Now came the hard part. Taking a deep breath, Rebecca reached up and grabbed the edges of the opening in the ceiling. How did Bones do this? She was much shorter than he was, and though she could reach the ceiling easily, she couldn't get any leverage to pull herself through the opening.

She tried again, jumping and attempting to get her elbows up over the edge, but it didn't work. Once more, and then she looked up through the hole. "I can't do it," she gasped.

Bones looked down at her for a long moment. Then, "Move!" he commanded. As she got out of his way, he swung down and dropped onto the floor. "Stand up there!" he snapped at her. Rebecca stepped up again onto the toilet seat and Bones bent and put his arms around her lower legs. Grunting slightly, he lifted her up. Her shoulders reached the level of the ceiling and she extended her arms onto the floor of the attic.

"Okay!" she called breathlessly, and pulled herself through the opening. She scrambled out of his way as he followed.

An old backpack leaned against the wall by the small window, and Rebecca stuffed her purse into it on top of the blanket and the food Bones had already packed. The extra blanket wouldn't fit, but it didn't matter—she'd probably use it to wrap up Ethan anyway.

Now that she looked at it, the window was tiny. Would she and Bones be able to wriggle through it? But he was already pushing it open—it swung sideways on hinges, like a little door. Cold air blew into the attic, carrying snowflakes that melted on Rebecca's hot face.

Bones put both feet out the window and pushed his body partway through until he was sitting on the sill. The edge of his jacket caught on the window frame, but he yanked it clear. Twisting around so he lay with his belly on the sill, he pushed himself outward, holding on to the frame with both hands. His shoulders were a tight squeeze but he worked them through, dropping to dangle below the level of the window. Then Rebecca saw his hands loosen their grip and let go.

She rushed to the window and stuck her head out. Bones had landed on the overhang that formed a small protected area in front of the cabin. It sloped down away from the cabin wall, but the snow was apparently wet enough so he hadn't slid off onto the ground. Now he looked up at her. "Drop the kid."

Rebecca turned to Ethan, who looked groggy enough to fall asleep on the spot. He didn't seem surprised or even interested in the fact that he was up here in the attic. Worried, Rebecca wondered if they should stay here and forget about escaping. What if Ethan caught pneumonia or something awful like that? But they *couldn't* stay here, not after the vague and terrifying threats Mr. Underwood had been muttering last night.

She pulled Ethan's mittens onto his hands and zipped up his jacket as close around his neck as she could. Then she said, "Okay, Ethan, I'm going to help you climb out the window and Bones is going to catch you. Let's go, sweetie."

The child looked alarmed and hung back when she took his hand. But Rebecca hustled him over to the little window and helped him get his legs through the opening until his stomach rested on the edge. With her own hands under his armpits, she pushed him slowly outward, leaning out the window herself and holding him away from the wall. Below her Bones held out his arms. "Go ahead, I'm ready."

Forcing a smile for Ethan, she leaned out as far as she could and lowered her hands. Then, her heart beating fast, she let go. The drop wasn't a long one, but she didn't breathe until she saw him safe in Bones's embrace.

Hardly pausing, Bones turned and strode to the front of the overhang. Rebecca saw him sit Ethan down on the edge and then begin to slide his own legs over the side. But she didn't have time to watch any more. Quickly she tossed the backpack out the window. It bounced on the far edge of the overhang and down to the ground below. Next came the extra blanket and the heavy old jacket— if she put it on, she was afraid she wouldn't fit through the window.

Rebecca looked around the attic. No, there was nothing else that had to go with them. Taking a deep breath, she put one foot in its oversized boot through the window, followed by the other. Wriggling clumsily, she edged her way outward, and then stopped for a moment. This was pretty scary—what if she couldn't . . . Don't think about it, she whispered angrily to herself, just do it!

Twisting around to lie on her belly, the way Bones had done it, she pushed her body backward. When her shoulders were through she dangled for a moment, grasping the window frame. But she couldn't get a good grip with her gloves on, and she slipped down, bumping her chin hard on the sill and landing on all fours on the snowy overhang.

Her eyes smarting with tears, Rebecca rubbed her chin gently and winced. But she was out! She crawled to the edge and saw Bones waiting for her, with Ethan still in his arms. This next drop looked easy, compared with what she'd just done. Without hesitating, she turned on her stomach, slid her feet out as far as she could, and pushed herself off.

CHAPTER SIXTEEN

Standing in front of the cabin, Rebecca realized for the first time how hard it was snowing. This looked like a major snowstorm, the kind that caused big traffic problems as drivers skidded and slid on the roads. Maybe Mr. Underwood wouldn't be able to get back up the road to the cabin.

Even as that thought went through her mind, Rebecca knew it wouldn't do her any good. So what if Ethan's father couldn't drive back here? Now that she and the little boy were out of the cabin, they had to get to shelter of some kind as soon as possible. And it wasn't going to be easy. She wouldn't be able to walk very fast through the deepening snowdrifts. Her heart sank as she thought, Ethan won't be able to walk at all. He doesn't have boots on, only sneakers, and besides, he's so small and the snow is too deep. But I don't think I can carry him far. Trudging through this heavy snow with a child in my arms or on my back will wear me out in no time. Thank goodness Bones is here.

Rebecca picked up the large old jacket she'd tossed to the ground and shook it, sending snowflakes flying. As she pulled it on and struggled with the zipper, she looked at Bones. His dark eyes were fixed on her and his brows were drawn together in an impatient frown.

The minute she lifted the backpack from the snow and shrugged her arms into it, he spoke. "Okay, Rebecca, I'm out of here." He paused and then added awkwardly, "Hope you and the kid find the cops and they catch that sucker and put him away." He held Ethan out toward her. "You gonna carry him or what? He don't have no boots on."

Rebecca stared at Bones, her eyes filled with dismay. "Oh, Bones, you've got to help us! I don't think I can carry him very far by myself, and we've got to get away from here and get him to a doctor. Won't you help me take him to whatever the nearest town is? Please?"

But the tall boy was shaking his head vehemently. "Uh-uh, no way, I ain't going into no town around here—get sent back to St. Ignatius, no thank you! I can't give you no more help, Rebecca, I got to get out of here and up to Canada."

One part of Rebecca's brain was thinking with total irrelevance, *Isn't it odd how Bones sometimes talks that ungrammatical street-talk way and sometimes not? It's like he's got two different* languages and he switches back and forth. At the same time she was frantically trying to come up with an idea that would help her and Ethan get away. Obviously Bones was afraid to come with them anywhere that people might be on the lookout for him—a runaway from whatever kind of place St. Ignatius was—and she couldn't really blame him. But how was she going to get Ethan to safety?

The extra blanket was still lying on the ground. It's not going to work to make a sling to carry Ethan in—he'll still be too heavy for me in this snow, she thought. But could I drag it behind me like a sled with him wrapped up in it?

She dismissed the idea immediately—the blanket would be soaking wet in a matter of moments and Ethan would freeze. But a sled would be perfect.

"Okay," she said to Bones, "if you won't come with us, you won't. But you know we're not going to get far if I have to carry Ethan. I'm going to look in the shed and see if there's a sled or something I can pull him on. Please, just wait that long."

Before he could reply, she walked away, rounding the corner of the cabin. The snow was heavy, dragging on her big clumsy boots, and she could feel the pull on the muscles in her legs. Please, let there be a sled, or a toboggan, or something. Even a garbage-can lid would do, she thought, remembering her own childhood and the variety of objects she'd used to slide down snow-covered hills.

But when she pulled open the door of the shed, there was nothing inside but firewood. Rebecca blinked her eyes hard. She couldn't cry now. But what was she going to do?

Bones walked up behind her and peered into the little shed. He shook his head. "Nothing here that helps any."

"I've got to think of something!" Rebecca burst out. Wasn't there anything here that she could fashion into a makeshift sled? Certainly the logs were useless—too heavy and the wrong shape. But what about the boards the shed was built from? Could she pry a couple of them off somehow and tie them together?

Tie them with what? she asked herself as she walked around the outside of the little building, looking for loose boards. A few were obviously about ready to fall off the little building, but they were also obviously rotten and useless for her purpose. She trudged back to the doorway feeling discouraged.

Then inspiration struck. "The door!" Her voice was full of excitement. "It'll work, if we can just get it off its hinges!"

Her enthusiasm must have been contagious, because Bones sat Ethan carefully on a log inside the shed and then came to peer at the door's hinges. He grinned at Rebecca. "Easy as pie," he said. Taking a folding knife out of his pocket, he opened a short blade and stuck the end of it under the rim of the upper hinge pin. He wiggled the knife gently and then pulled the hinge pin up and out.

In another moment he had the lower one out, too, and the door lay flat on the snow.

"Now, how you going to pull it?" Bones asked.

It was a good question. Rebecca gazed around the inside of the shed, but there was still nothing there but logs for the fire. Ethan looked up at her. "Becca, I'm cold." His voice held an unfamiliar note of whining, and Rebecca felt a pang of remorse. She'd been so busy worrying about everything else that she'd forgotten the child was sick and in need of special care.

"Of course you are, sweetie," she told him. "Let's wrap you up in this nice warm blanket." As she spoke she opened up the blanket and spread it on the floor of the shed, then set the little boy in the middle of it and pulled it up and around him. And then she thought, *Of course, I can cut strips off one of these blankets and use them instead of rope.*

She explained her plan to Bones, and he nodded. "Okay, but let's hurry it up, I want to get going before it gets dark."

Alarmed, Rebecca peered at the sky. It was gray and completely overcast, almost invisible through the snow that still fell heavily. She had no idea what time it was, but what if Mr. Underwood was on his way back right this minute, trying to get to the cabin before the roads were impassable?

Again she felt desperate to get away. She dug the other blanket out of the backpack and Bones began cutting a wide strip off one end of it. But it was slow going. The wool fabric wouldn't rip, and sawing at it with a knife took forever. Rebecca held the two cut edges taut and Bones sliced with the knife.

When they finally had a long strip of blanket material, a new problem confronted them. How could it be attached to the door? There was nothing to tie it to. At last they agreed that the only solution was to make a notch in each side of the door near one end, then tie a wool strip around the door at the notched place and tie a pulling cord to it.

Long agonizing minutes went by as Rebecca waited for Bones to carve out the notches and then helped him cut off two more strips of blanket. Any second she expected to see the headlights of Mr. Underwood's car climbing up the drive. Fantastic scenes flashed through her mind. Maybe Bones would help her hit the man over the head with one of these logs and then tie him up with the strips of blanket. But what if somehow he got hold of Ethan and threatened to hurt him? What if he had a gun she didn't know about? Oh, they just had to get out of here!

At last the two "ropes" were attached to the sled. Using the third strip of blanket, Rebecca tied the backpack onto the door near the back end—it would give Ethan something to lean against.

Still swathed in the other blanket, the child gazed at her with heavy-lidded eyes. Rebecca picked him up. "Ethan, listen to me. You're going to sit on this door, like a sled, and I'm going to pull you, okay?" As she talked to him she carried him outside and put him on the sled, tucking the remains of the cut-up blanket around him. At least he was warm enough for the time being. "All right, Ethan, here we go!"

Rebecca pulled on the woolen "rope." It stretched in her hands without budging the door, and then quite suddenly the primitive sled began to move, knocking Ethan off balance. Wrapped like a mummy in the blankets, he couldn't put out a hand to save himself, and Rebecca realized that she had to rearrange things.

In a fever of anxiety she untied the strip she had used to attach the backpack to the sled. Unwrapping Ethan's cocoon of blankets, she set the backpack on top of the blanket just behind Ethan and then tied it down to the sled again. It meant she couldn't tuck the blankets around the little boy as tightly as they had been before, but there was no other way she could think of to keep him on the sled and still able to move his limbs a bit.

That's as good as I'm going to get it, Rebecca thought finally. She stood up and took hold of the sled's pull rope again. With an attempt at a cheerful smile, she said brightly, "Okay, let's try it again!"

This time the sled started without a jerk and she dragged it behind her around the cabin to the front. Without runners like a real sled, it didn't slide very smoothly, and it was a heavy weight to pull. Still, it was certainly lots better than trying to carry Ethan on her own.

Bones walked beside her, his close-cropped dark

hair matted with snow that dribbled down his forehead as it melted. Rebecca's hair was wet, too, and she thought fleetingly, I hope I don't start to get sick myself. But so far her feet were dry in the enormous boots.

Dragging the sled, Rebecca trudged down the long curving drive that led away from the cabin, her mind churning with a million unanswerable questions. What if Mr. Underwood was coming up the drive right now? Would she hear the car soon enough to yank the sled into the trees and hide? Wouldn't he see the tracks they were leaving? There were so many things to worry about, she couldn't focus on a single one.

When they were near the end of the drive, they could see a road below them, and Rebecca remembered the narrow dirt road Mr. Underwood had driven along—was it only three days ago? Bones stopped and turned to look at Rebecca. "I been thinking," he said. "That road down there has got to be the only way to this place, and we don't know which way the kid's dad went on it." He gave Rebecca a questioning look. When she nodded, he went on. "So, it won't be smart for you to walk on that road. Ain't no telling when he'll come back, and ain't no place to hide if you're in the road. I think you better go through the woods. If you go that way"—he pointed into the trees, and Rebecca followed his gesture—"you'll meet up with the main highway after a while, and then you'll be able to find some folks to help you."

Rebecca looked into his serious face. His idea made sense—she would be more vulnerable to getting spotted and caught by Mr. Underwood if she followed the dirt road. But setting off into the woods by herself with a sick child to take care of was a prospect that filled her with dread. Maybe she could still persuade Bones to come with them. "What are you going to do, Bones?"

He waved his hand in the opposite direction. "What I told you—I'm heading for Canada."

"Won't you just—" But before she could finish the sentence, Bones was shaking his head.

"No, no, I told you, I can't take the chance of meeting up with some cop type and getting myself shipped right back to where I just got out of. I'm out and I'm going to make sure I stay that way."

"But, Bones, don't you see? If you help us, you'll be a hero, with articles in the newspapers and who knows what else. Then no one will be able to send you back to reform school or whatever it is. And I'm sure my parents and Ethan's mom will do anything they possibly can to help you. Please, Bones, don't run away."

He stared at Rebecca for a long moment without speaking, while fat snowflakes landed gently on his face and hair and melted into water drops. Then he smiled slightly. "Oh, no, Rebecca, you can't sweet-talk me that way. Ain't nobody going to help me but myself, 'specially not no white folks probably never seen a black face before. But I know you meant it for real, so—well, thanks anyway."

There was nothing more she could say to change his mind. But she couldn't just let him disappear forever—she didn't even know his last name! "Okay, Bones." She sighed. "You do what you've got to do. But please, call me or write to me when you get to Canada—wait, let me give you my address." Quickly she burrowed into the backpack and found a pen in her purse, but there was nothing to write on. Yanking a dollar out of her wallet, she wrote *Rebecca Harper* and then her address and phone number.

She handed the bill to Bones. "Can you read it?" she asked anxiously. When he nodded, she said, trying to make a joke, "Just don't spend it before you copy it on something else! And Bones—what's your last name?"

He looked startled, then grinned. "Thomas. My real name is James Thomas, but they always called me Bones 'cause I'm so skinny." He glanced down the drive. "Time to get moving, before that man comes back." His voice softened as he said awkwardly, "You take care now, hear?"

Rebecca swallowed hard. "I will—and you take care, too. Good luck, Bones. And thank you for helping us escape."

He looked into her eyes for another space of time. Then he turned away and began to walk steadily into the trees. In seconds he had vanished.

A feeling of desolation swept over Rebecca. As his tall figure was swallowed up by the snow-laden trees, she stood rooted to the spot. How could she possibly get herself and Ethan to safety?

CHAPTER SEVENTEEN

In Marian Underwood's kitchen, Sergeant Van Kerelin hung up the phone. He looked around at the anxious group of people who had been listening intently to his side of the conversation with Chief Petievich of the Porterville police. "I guess you heard most of that," he told them, "but let me run through it so you all know what's going on."

Marian nodded quickly, her face pinched with fear. Ellen Harper clutched her husband's hand tighter with one hand, and with the other reached out to Kathy Delarra, who sat on her other side.

Van tried to smile reassuringly at all of them, but his voice was serious. "Well, after this second phone call, we know for sure that your former husband is the person who kidnapped Ethan and Rebecca. We were able to trace the call, and it was made from a pay phone at a rest stop on the

New York Thruway, up around Little Falls, about thirty miles east of Utica. The state police are sending a car over there to see if anyone noticed him, but I think it's a good bet they won't find out anything useful. So, what I need to ask you, Mrs. Underwood, is whether your ex-husband had any connections in that part of New York."

Marian shook her head hopelessly. "Not that I know of," she said. "But after all, I've had hardly any contact with him for more than three years—since before Ethan was born."

Ellen and Bob Harper exchanged a glance. Van Kerelin went on, "Well, let me know if you come up with any ideas. Where he called from is up there near the southern edge of Adirondack Park, and that whole section of the state is pretty deserted in the winter except for a few small ski areas. There are houses and cabins scattered all around, but most of them are closed up until spring."

"Are you people planning to search that whole area?" Bob Harper asked. "I mean, he made it pretty clear that he didn't want any police to be involved."

Van nodded. "Yes, and that's why we're definitely keeping a low profile and not doing anything obvious like sending out the helicopters. We don't want to scare the guy into anything he'd regret later. Besides, it's snowing steadily up there—they wouldn't be able to fly now even if they wanted to."

Bob glanced at the window. Porterville was more than one hundred miles south of the Adirondack

Park, but big fat snowflakes were smacking into the windowpane. What was it like where Harley Underwood was holding Rebecca and Ethan hostage? Bob's eyes met those of Van Kerelin for a long moment, but the sergeant's expression was unreadable.

"But why is he doing this?" Ellen burst out. "It's his own child—why would he want to hurt him?"

"Because he wants to hurt me." Tears filled Marian's eyes as she looked at Ellen. "I'm so sorry that Rebecca got caught in all this—I never imagined that Harley would do something so terrible. In fact, I never thought Ethan or I would see him again." She brushed the tears from her cheeks and went on unsteadily, "It's hard to explain about Harley. He's a brilliant person, trained as an electrical engineer, and he's also an inventor. When we met he had a great job with a company that was working on new technology for burning fuel cleaner and things like that, and he was pretty happy there. But then he invented some little gizmo and he felt the company didn't give him credit for it and just took it over for themselves. He was very bitter and angry, and he quit his job. By that time we were married and Ethan was on the way."

Marian sighed and took a sip of the now cold coffee in her mug. Rebecca's mother looked at the other woman in sympathy. It must be hard for Marian to tell us all this, she thought, and relive what must have been a very unhappy time. She shivered involuntarily as she tried to imagine how she would feel if the man she'd been married to and the father of her only child had done what Harley Underwood had. And where was he now, with Ethan and Rebecca?

Taking a deep breath, Marian continued. "Anyway, it seemed as if Harley was getting angrier and angrier and more and more strange, and he began to think that the whole world was against him, and that I was, too. I didn't know how to deal with the situation, and finally it got to the point where he got so angry with me that he hit me and knocked me down. And I couldn't think of anything else to do to help him, so I left."

"This was before Ethan was born?" Sergeant Kerelin asked. When Marian nodded, he added, "And you haven't seen him since?"

"Well, of course I let him know when Ethan was born. He called a couple of times to say he wanted to see the baby, but then he didn't follow up. The only time I saw him was when Ethan was about a year old—we met at the zoo and spent about an hour together. And that was all. I guess I hoped I'd never have anything to do with him again."

"What about custody of Ethan? Was there any discussion of it between you?" Van Kerelin's voice was carefully neutral.

"Oh, no," Marian told him, "he never brought it up. I don't think he could see himself caring for a child. We made a clean break—he doesn't pay child support and he doesn't have any formal visitation rights. And I think after I left, he got even more reclusive and peculiar. About a year after he quit his job, the place where he had worked burned down, and I always wondered . . ." Her voice trailed off.

"But this phone call—" Ellen leaned forward. "It sounded as if he wants to have Ethan with him and he thinks you're keeping his child away from him."

"I know." Marian spread her hands helplessly. "I don't understand it."

"Sounds to me as if he's been stewing over his problems and getting weirder by the minute, and now he's gone off the deep end." Bob Harper stared directly at Sergeant Kerelin. "But that doesn't help you find him, does it?"

Van looked around the table at all of them. "At least we know his general location now. And everything we learn about him helps fill in the picture." He tried to make his voice convey reassurance. "Our first priority is the safety of Ethan and Rebecca. And don't forget, he said he'd call back to arrange about the money. So we have some time."

Kathy Delarra put her arm around her friend's shoulders. "Don't worry, Ellen, the police will find them. And I'm sure the children are okay—you heard them yesterday on the phone."

Ellen Harper tried to believe her. But yesterday seemed like a long time ago, and Rebecca's voice had only been on a tape even then. Who could tell when that tape had been made? The more Ellen learned about Harley Underwood, the more terrified she felt. The man was unstable and dangerous, and her daughter and Marian's son were still in his clutches.

CHAPTER EIGHTEEN

Rebecca trudged through the snow, pausing now and then to wipe the moisture off her forehead with a gloved hand. It wasn't exactly walking, it was more like sinking at every step into a deep hole, and it was incredibly hard work. If there was a path through these woods, she couldn't see it. Her only option was to choose the spaces between the trees that looked most promising, and sometimes these spaces were deceptive. They appeared open and easy to get through, but in fact the snow concealed tangles of bushes and vines that caught at her feet and blocked the way, forcing her to back up and try another route.

She was grateful for the big waterproof boots she had found in the cabin. Without them her feet would be soaking wet and probably frost-bitten. But they certainly weren't easy to walk in. She felt as if she was lifting a hundred-pound weight with each step, and the paper towels she had stuffed in them to keep them on her feet were now wadded up uncomfortably under her insteps. The jacket, too, got heavier and heavier as it absorbed more and more moisture, and her shoulders began to ache under this extra burden. Still, she couldn't take it off and do without the protection it provided. Her own short jacket and jeans would be drenched in a minute, and the thought of that cold wet fabric against her skin make her shiver.

Rebecca halted for a moment and transferred the pull rope of the sled to her other hand. If it were longer, she could put it around her waist and lean into it to drag the sled. Even if it were possible, though, she wasn't sure that method would work. But the muscles in her arms were trembling from exertion and it hurt to twist one arm and shoulder backward as she plodded along with the sled behind her.

This stupid sled! she thought. It seemed to Rebecca to have a mind of its own, and not a very nice one. It caught on every twig, every vine, every branch of every bush, not to mention the rocks that were hidden under the snow and the trees that were not quite far enough apart to let the sled through easily. She swore under her breath as she went back for the millionth time to dislodge a stubborn whippy branch that was caught on the sled's front corner.

It was dark here in the woods under the trees. In some places they formed a loose-woven canopy that kept some of the snow from falling on Rebecca and Ethan, but she had learned that it only took the gentlest brush against a towering evergreen to loosen an avalanche from its boughs. That had already happened twice, and she'd had to stop and sweep the heavy snow off the sled and off Ethan's blankets with her gloves.

She was getting even more worried about Ethan. He seemed to have retreated into a private place. For a while she had wondered if he'd fallen asleep, but when she looked back she saw his huge brown eyes gazing at her. There were dark shadows under them, and his face was so pale except for bright spots of color on each cheek.

Stopping again, Rebecca picked up a handful of the clean snow and put some in her mouth. She was sweating in spite of the cold air. It took enormous amounts of energy to wade through the deep wet snow and to haul the heavy sled with Ethan on it behind her. How far had she come? And how much farther would she have to go before she came to the highway and civilization? She had no idea.

She walked perhaps another ten minutes, and then Rebecca knew she had to rest. Pushing up her jacket sleeve to check her watch, she saw that it was only a little after three. But the lowering gray sky and the relentlessly falling snow made it seem much later, and much darker than it should be.

Rebecca knew she should keep going. If she and Ethan were still in these woods when evening came, they'd be in big trouble. The overcast sky would block out any light from moon or stars, and she'd be totally lost.

But she was so tired. Bits of stories about snowbound travelers swirled through her memory. Words like exhaustion, dehydration, starvation created a kind of rhythmic chant in her head. Maybe she should stop and build a shelter of snowdrifts, like the snow forts she remembered constructing as a little kid. They could lie on the sled and the blankets would keep them warm enough, she thought. Then in the morning, when she wasn't so exhausted, they could go on.

The idea was so tempting that Rebecca began to look around for a big tree that would shield them from the blowing snow or for a tangle of overgrown bushes they could burrow into for protection. But then she thought, Wait a minute, let's think this through. How much farther can it be until I hit the highway—five miles or so, maybe a little more? The numbers were just guesses, because she actually had no idea how far she would have to walk through the woods.

A more important question was how far she had already come from the cabin. It would be terrible to stop and make a shelter, only to have Mr. Underwood find them and drag them back to captivity. Besides, even if he didn't manage to find them today, they would be just as visible tomorrow. She couldn't count on finding people right away even when she got to the highway. This part of the state was not heavily populated, especially in the winter, and the snowstorm would keep most sane residents off the roads and snug at home. So if Mr. Underwood started cruising the highway and searching for Rebecca and Ethan in the morning, he'd spot them in a minute.

Rebecca gave a frustrated sigh. She couldn't make up her mind what was the best thing to do. Glancing down at Ethan, she was shaken to find that he was staring listlessly at the ground next to his sled. Normally he would be talking to her, pointing out interesting sights or asking for something to eat. This unnaturally passive state wasn't like him at all, and it troubled her deeply.

I'll have to keep going, she thought. Dropping to her knees in front of the child, she said, "Ethan? How are you doing, sweetie?"

He looked at her without a smile. "Okay," he answered softly. "But, Becca, I want to go home."

"I know," she told him. "I do, too!" Her voice held more emotion than she had intended, and she added quickly, "Are you thirsty, Ethan? Do you want to lick some snow and let it melt in your mouth?"

"Okay," he said again. He watched as Rebecca gathered up a handful of the new-fallen snow and patted it into a rough lump. When she handed it to him, the little boy took a small taste. Then he set it down on the sled beside him.

Truly alarmed now, Rebecca gazed at Ethan. He must really be sick, not to be asking for something to eat or drink by now. What could she do for him, besides trying to reach shelter and help? Close to despair, she heard terrible words in her head: What if he dies? Maybe I've made him worse, bringing him out here in the cold. But we can't go back, she thought wildly. We can't!

She heard a soft noise behind her. Oh, please, no, it couldn't be Mr. Underwood! Rebecca stood up and whirled to face him, unconsciously shielding Ethan with her own body.

But it was Bones. Plodding slowly toward her in the path she had made, he raised one hand in silent greeting.

"Bones!" Rebecca breathed. For a moment she felt confused. She had never expected to see him again. "Why—what are you—"

He had come up in front of her and now he looked from her face down to the child on the sled. "I couldn't do it," he said gruffly. "I figured you'd never make it by yourself—it's too tough walking through this stuff. So, well, I thought I better give you some help, at least as far as the highway."

Rebecca felt tears fill her eyes as she smiled at him. "Oh, Bones, you'll never know how happy I am to see you. I was about to give up."

"Yeah," he answered briefly, sounding almost embarrassed. "And you didn't get very far yet. Let's move."

Bones picked up the pull rope of the sled and started trudging forward. Blinking the moisture from her eyes, Rebecca followed. The sled packed down the snow somewhat, so it was a little easier to walk behind it than through the unbroken snow. But that didn't completely account for her renewed energy. It was the presence of another person to share the load that made her feel so much better.

They were making much faster progress than Rebecca had managed by herself. From her position behind the sled, she could see when it was about to run into something and could lean down and redirect it, or push it away from whatever it had hit. This saved all the time it had taken to stop, go back and dislodge the sled, and then return and pick up the rope again. They didn't talk much, only an occasional call of "Stop!" from Rebecca and then, after she'd straightened the sled, "Okay, go ahead."

Ethan's eyelids were drooping and Rebecca thought he might doze off. She pulled the blanket closer around his head and shoulders, hoping he was staying warm enough in spite of sitting so still.

Sometime later Bones stopped for a moment, rotating his shoulders and stretching his back with his hands over his head. "I'll pull for a while," Rebecca told him. As she picked up the rope and started off, she realized that night was already closing in. Unconsciously she tried to walk faster. She wanted to be out of the woods when darkness fell.

Suddenly she stumbled and nearly pitched forward into the snow. The makeshift rope had frayed where it rubbed against the wooden "sled" and it had parted, leaving Rebecca holding one end. Peering closely at it, Rebecca squatted down and tied the two frayed ends together. She couldn't help noticing that it was unraveling in several other places. Oh, just hold together until we get out of here! she thought.

When she stood up again, Bones said, "Look." He gestured through the trees in front of them and to the right. "See that light? That's a car on the highway."

Gazing where he pointed, Rebecca saw what he meant. A faint patch of light seemed to be moving, glowing erratically through the snow. She grinned thankfully. "Not much farther now," she said.

Bones smiled back at her. "Yeah." He took the pull rope from her hand and began trudging in the direction of the lights.

But it was another half hour at least before they could see the road a couple of hundred yards through the trees. It was only visible because a car was traveling slowly along it and they could see the nimbus of light its headlights created. After it had passed, the country road melted into its black surroundings again.

As they moved closer to the highway, Rebecca began to feel nervous. At last she called out to Bones, "Stop! Wait a minute." When he turned to look at her, she could hardly see his face in the dark. "Maybe we should stay in the trees—you know, walk parallel to the road but not so close that a driver could see us. I'm worried that Mr. Underwood will be out looking for us, especially if he got back and saw the tracks we left in the snow."

After a moment Bones replied, "No, it's better if we get to the road and walk along the edge of it. We'll go much faster than we can get through this deep snow. And don't worry—we'll see a car coming before it sees us 'cause we'll see the lights."

Rebecca sighed, not completely convinced. "I don't know, maybe you're right, but I still feel nervous about it."

"And besides, we got another problem," Bones said. "I think this rope is about to give out again. We may have to forget the sled pretty soon. And if I have to carry Ethan, it'll be an awful lot easier on the road."

Suddenly Rebecca realized that Bones was no longer talking about leaving once they reached the highway. Gratefully she thought, He's giving up his own chance of escaping to make sure we get to safety. I'm not sure I could do that if I were in his position. I guess he feels sort of responsible for us.

Aloud she said, "Okay, I guess that all makes sense. Let's hurry up and get onto the highway—

the sooner we're back to the real world, the better!"

The final stretch of deep snow through evergreens and close-packed groups of birches seemed endless, but at last they stood at the outer edge of the treeless space that ran along next to the road. It was lower than the roadway itself and for now they were invisible to any car that might pass. They'd seen only one set of lights go by, however, since they had started toward the highway. Obviously people weren't out traveling on this snowy night.

Rebecca and Bones stopped again, looking at the slope up to the highway. "Should we pull the sled up there or not?" Rebecca asked.

"Nah, it's not worth it," Bones replied. "If the road has been plowed, the sled won't go smoothly—it'll get stuck all the time. And it's not going to last much longer anyway." As he spoke he jerked on the fraying rope, and it broke immediately. "We're lucky it got this far," he said.

"Yes, we are," Rebecca agreed. "But let's think about how we're going to carry Ethan and the other stuff."

"We can eat the food now," Bones told her. And of course he was right. It would give them a much-needed energy boost, besides lightening the load that had to be carried. Rebecca dug out the peanut-butter-and-jelly sandwiches and handed one to Bones. She took a bite of another one herself, and then said to Ethan, "Hey, Ethan, do you want something to eat?"

But the little boy just shook his head, and no matter how Rebecca tried to coax him, he wasn't interested in eating. Her worry renewed, Rebecca gulped down the rest of the sticky sandwich and put one of the apples in her pocket. "Here," she said, handing the other one to Bones, "take this for later, and I'll leave the crackers in the backpack. I want to hurry as much as we can—I'm afraid Ethan is getting sicker."

"Okay," Bones said, swallowing the last of his bread, "give me one of those blankets. If he's sick, he needs to keep wrapped up and warm."

Rebecca unwound one of the blankets that sheltered Ethan and handed it to Bones. She sat on the sled and held Ethan close as she watched the tall boy try to wrap the blanket around himself in such a way that it would protect Ethan. He wasn't making much progress and Rebecca thought, There must be a simple way to do this. All those people in other cultures carry stuff in squares of cloth all the time. How do they do it?

And then it came to her as a sort of mental picture. Moving Ethan off her lap, she stood up. "Here," she said to Bones, "let me try." She folded the blanket diagonally to make a doubled triangle and put it around Bones's waist with the fold at the bottom and the point up toward his chin. At the back she crossed the two other points and handed them to Bones over his shoulders. "Hold these," she commanded.

Picking up Ethan, she handed him to Bones, who held the child against his chest. Ethan's arms went around Bones's neck and his legs around Bones's waist, covered by the blanket. Now Rebecca tied the blanket corners together at Bones's shoulders, attaching one of the front corner layers to the left end Bones was holding and the other to the right.

Meanwhile Bones put his arms around Ethan, supporting his bottom. "Pull that side up a little more," he told Rebecca. "Okay, that's good. We're ready to roll."

Rebecca hurriedly stuffed the other blanket into the backpack—she was reluctant to abandon it, in case they ended up sitting somewhere in the snow and cold—and shrugged her arms into the backpack's straps. "Okay," she told Bones, "let's go."

It wasn't easy to scramble up the slippery snow-covered slope to the highway with the big boots on her feet and the pack on her back. And it was even harder for Bones, with nothing to help him keep his balance and the weight of the little boy in the homemade carrying sling. We should have waited to get Ethan settled until we climbed up here, Rebecca thought, but it was too late now. Finally she evolved a method of climbing ahead two or three steps, digging her feet into the hillside, and reaching back to take Bones's hand and steady him as he tried to climb the short distance.

At last they stood panting on the shoulder of the highway. Now what? Rebecca thought, and realized that she had no idea which way the closest town lay. She peered in both directions, trying to distinguish a glow that would indicate human habitation. But the overcast sky and the still-falling snow made it impossible to see more than a few hundred yards in any direction.

She looked at Bones. "Which way?"

He laughed shortly. "I don't know, but I pick that way," gesturing to his right. "Want to flip a coin?"

"Nope," Rebecca answered. "We'll try your way. How's Ethan doing?" she added. The child's passive silence bothered her more and more. It was so unlike the cheerful child she knew, who had even managed to keep chatting with her during their imprisonment in the cabin.

Bones peered down at the little boy's face huddled against his shoulder. "He's okay, I guess. Might be asleep."

Rebecca took off her glove and put her hand against Ethan's cheek. His skin felt cold to her touch. "Oh, Bones, we've got to get him to a doctor or something soon!"

"Yeah, well, let's go then."

Side by side they set off. The highway had been plowed sometime fairly recently. To their right, on the shoulder, was an uneven mound left by the plow. It was about a foot high, and sometimes more. But on the road itself the snow was only a couple of inches deep, and they plodded along at a steady pace.

They might have been on the moon or at the North Pole, Rebecca thought. There was no sign of life other than themselves, and no sign yet of civilization—no streetlights, no houses, no cars.

And it was absolutely silent. It was eerie and a bit frightening, but oddly exhilarating, too, and she would have enjoyed it under other circumstances. Now, though, she kept squinting along the highway, hoping to see an indication of warmth and help for Ethan.

And then, behind them, there was a faint rhythmic sound. It had to be a car—the noise was snow chains on the tires hitting the road surface at regular intervals. Rebecca spun around, and saw a faint cloud of light some way back.

"There's a car coming!" she said to Bones. "Let's stop it and hitchhike. We've got to get Ethan indoors and call a doctor for him!"

"No, Rebecca, don't do it!" Bones's voice was sharp. "It's probably Ethan's father, and who knows if he has a gun or something. Just hide until he goes by. We'll get to a town soon, I know we will."

Following his own advice, Bones stepped awkwardly over the snow piled up by the snowplow. Standing on the other side of it, he extended his hand to help Rebecca.

The car was getting closer. Now Rebecca could see its headlights instead of just a diffused glow. Hesitating, she stood on the highway. What if Bones was right and it was Mr. Underwood in the car? She took a step toward Bones.

But no, he must have returned to the cabin hours ago, and he was probably following their trail on foot through the woods. What were the chances of this being his car? It was much more likely to be somebody else, somebody who could help them. And if they kept walking, it might take hours to find a house with people in it—maybe it was mostly summer places around here, like the cabin, and they could waste precious time knocking on doors where no one was home. And besides, Ethan was getting worse and worse.

Still torn with indecision, Rebecca watched the car coming closer. Should she wave and flag it down, or not? She couldn't yet distinguish the shape or color of the car, but suddenly, irrationally, she felt certain that Bones was right. It was Mr. Underwood, out searching for her and Ethan! She had to hide!

But as she turned to climb over the heaped-up snow, the car's headlights caught her full in their glare. Rebecca looked back at the car once more. She heard the note of its engine change, and the rhythm of the tires' chains grew faster. The driver had speeded up his car, and it was coming straight toward Rebecca!

CHAPTER NINETEEN

Terrified, Rebecca stood for a moment, transfixed in the glare of the oncoming headlights. Then she heard Bones yelling at her. "Rebecca! Move!"

She turned and ran toward him. The snow that was heaped up at the side of the highway was between them. Rebecca stumbled and nearly fell. But Bones was reaching across the mound of snow, and she grabbed at the hand he stretched out to her. Clinging to it as if to a lifeline, she scrambled over the piled-up snow. Quickly Bones yanked her toward him, and then, keeping an eye on the oncoming car, he pulled her farther along the shoulder. The car sped past them, skidding crazily and bouncing off the snow pile at the place where Rebecca had just been standing. It kept going, careening away from Rebecca and Bones down the wrong lane of the highway.

Shaken, Rebecca stood panting, still clutching Bones's hand. His other hand was pressing Ethan against his chest, and Rebecca caught a glimpse of the little boy's scared face. Then, looking back, she caught her breath with a gasp. The car was sliding across the highway in a U-turn that looked completely out of control. Rebecca waited for the crash she felt sure was coming, for the car to slam into the trees that came right down to the highway's opposite verge.

But the driver was incredibly lucky. The car straightened out without hitting anything and came to a stop for a moment, facing back the way it had come. Then the tires screamed, spinning in the snow, as the driver stepped on the accelerator. Picking up speed, the car hurtled toward them again, holding them in the bright tunnel of its headlights like butterflies impaled on mounting pins.

If she hadn't known before, Rebecca was certain now: The driver of the car was Mr. Underwood, and he was trying to kill all of them. It was her fault, she knew. If she had hidden when Bones told her to and had let the car go by, they would all be safe now, instead of standing immobilized in the path of a deadly juggernaut.

All this flashed through her mind in an instant. And then she felt herself knocked off her feet. Bones, still holding Ethan tight against his body with one hand and protecting the child's head with the other, cannoned into her full tilt. She fell, and Bones and Ethan fell on top of her.

Their momentum carried them over the lip of the embankment and they rolled, banging and bumping, down the slope to the gully at the bottom.

Lying in the snow, Rebecca heard above them the shriek of the car's engine as it was pushed to its limit. Then, as she watched, the car launched itself over the edge of the highway. It seemed to fly through the air for a moment, almost as if it would sprout wings like the cars in cartoons on TV. But this was real life. Plunging through space, the car aimed straight for the massive trunk of a tall pine that stood surrounded by smaller trees.

The sound of the impact was deafening in the silent landscape. As Rebecca looked on in horror, the pine tree snapped in two and its upper half fell slowly to the snow-covered forest floor. The car dropped to earth with a splintering crash that shook the ground where Rebecca and Bones lay, mesmerized by the car's trajectory. And then, as they watched, it burst into flame.

This can't be happening, Rebecca thought, it must be a made-for-TV movie. But she knew it was reality—the man who had been driving that car and trying to run her and Bones and Ethan down was trapped in an inescapable inferno. A mixture of horror, pity, and relief flooded through her.

Then she heard noises—ordinary sounds of a car door slamming and people talking excitedly—that brought her scrambling to her feet. In a moment she saw two figures at the top of the embankment, their bodies silhouetted by the lights of their car.

"Look at that!"

"Should we go down there and—"

"No, I don't think anyone could have survived a crash like that. Poor souls. Let's go on into town and notify the police, if they haven't been called out already."

They turned away, and Rebecca thought desperately, They're leaving! "Wait!" she cried, her voice cracking. "Please, wait!"

The man and the woman looked back, and Rebecca waved her arms frantically. "Look, Frank," the woman said, "there's someone down there!"

"Please help us!" Rebecca called. "We need help!"

By now Bones was sitting up, still cradling Ethan in his arms, and by the time the man and woman had slithered down the embankment, he was standing beside Rebecca.

The man gazed at them in astonishment. "How in the world did you manage to get out of that car?"

"We weren't in the car," Rebecca said, "we were walking, trying to get to a town, and he tried to run us over. See, he kidnapped us, or at least me and Ethan, and then we got away, and we were trying—" She broke off in confusion, her teeth chattering and her whole body trembling uncontrollably.

"It's a long story," Bones said to the man and woman who looked completely bewildered. "But the little boy is sick, and we need to get him to a doctor. Do you think you can—"

"Of course!" the woman cried. "You poor things, let's get you into the car where you can get warm."

Once again they climbed up the snowy embankment, this time assisted by helping hands. At the top Rebecca turned around. The car was still burning, but the flames were lower now, not reaching up into the branches as they had at first. The air was full of a dreadful smell. With a convulsive shudder Rebecca walked to the waiting car and climbed into the backseat with Bones. Reaching over, she pushed away the edge of the blanket that covered Ethan and took the child's hand in hers.

CHAPTER TWENTY

A week had passed, and for Rebecca life was beginning to settle back into its normal routines. The first few days after their escape had been full of activity, so much that it was confusing to keep track of what was going on.

To begin with, the Wartons (the couple who had picked up Rebecca, Ethan, and Bones beside the highway) had driven them into the nearby village of Elgar Lake. Rebecca insisted that the first thing she had to do was get Ethan to a doctor, and the Wartons took them all to the local clinic. While Mr. Warton called the police, Dr. Williams beckoned them into an examining room. Mrs. Warton followed Rebecca and Bones, who still hadn't let go of Ethan.

Dr. Williams smiled impartially at the little group. "What seems to be the problem?"

"This is Ethan," Mrs. Warton told her, gesturing toward the child, "and he has a fever, we think."

"Well, let's take a look." Dr. Williams took Ethan from Bones's arms and sat him on the examining table. A few minutes later she looked at Mrs. Warton. "His temperature isn't very high, only a little over a hundred. How long has he had the fever?"

Rebecca answered, "Since yesterday, I'm pretty sure, but I didn't have a thermometer."

Dr. Williams looked puzzled, but she finished her examination and then said, "It doesn't look like anything serious. I think it's a virus, maybe flu, and what he needs is lots of rest and TLC."

"Oh, good!" Rebecca felt as if a heavy weight had just been lifted off her shoulders. "I was so worried about him!"

Dr. Williams said slowly, "Are you the child's mother?"

Rebecca shook her head and then she haltingly explained the whole story, prompted by Mrs. Warton. By the time she stopped talking, Rebecca was drained. Her legs were trembling and she felt as if she needed to sit down. In a shaky voice she asked, "Can I use your phone to call my parents? They don't even know we're okay."

"Of course." Dr. Williams looked slightly stunned. "There's a phone right out there in the reception area."

Rebecca dialed the familiar number of her home and clutched the receiver hard as she listened to the ringing. At last her mother picked up. "Hello?"

"Mom?" Rebecca's voice wavered. "Mom, it's me, Rebecca, I'm okay, in fact everything's okay now."

"Oh, thank God!" Rebecca could hear her mother gulping back tears as she called out, "Bob! Bob, it's Rebecca!"

After that everything merged into a blur of talk and activity. Somehow Rebecca and Bones managed to explain their story to Sergeant Lionni of the state police, and then to Rebecca's parents and to Ethan's mother when they arrived a few hours later. There was a lot of coming and going by the police, and Rebecca overheard snatches of conversation about Mr. Underwood's crashed car and their efforts to get in touch with someone named Crockett who owned the cabin in the woods.

Sergeant Lionni spent a long time on the phone with Sergeant Van Kerelin in Porterville. When he hung up, he looked at Rebecca and Bones. "I have a good many questions I want to ask you both," he said, "but I think maybe you've had enough for tonight." He turned to Mr. and Mrs. Harper. "Will you be staying in this area for the night or—"

"Oh, no," Rebecca's mother said decisively. "We're going right home." She looked over at Marian Underwood, who sat with Ethan in her lap and her arms enclosing him as if she'd never let him go. "All right with you?" Marian nodded in agreement.

"Well, and what are we going to do with you?" Sergeant Lionni's eyes were fixed speculatively on Bones's face.

For a moment no one spoke, and the silence stretched out until Rebecca couldn't bear it. "You can't send him back to that place, St. Whatever," she said earnestly. "I mean, he saved our lives! Without him Ethan and I would be up in the woods freezing to death, or—" She broke off and shuddered at a mental image of Mr. Underwood pursuing them, following their tracks through the snow.

Her father put his hand on hers. "Okay, honey, don't get upset." To the sergeant he said, "The boy can come home with us, at least for now. We'll be responsible for him until—well, until things get straightened out." He looked at Bones, who had so far said very little and who was slouched in a chair with a scared and defiant look on his face. "That all right with you, son?"

Startled, Bones looked into the man's eyes, and then he smiled. "Yes, sure, that's fine." He paused and then added, "Thanks."

At that moment a young man came into the police building and began asking where the kidnap victims were. He was a reporter from the regional newspaper, and Rebecca wondered how he knew they were there. Later she realized that news reporters monitor the police frequencies on the radio, and he must have learned about the story that way. He was only the first of several reporters, from newspapers and radio and even TV, and although it was kind of exciting at first, eventually they all got tired of answering the same questions over and over.

On the drive home Rebecca recounted the whole story again for her parents, remembering new details and hearing for the first time what they had thought and felt through those terrible nights and days. When they finally reached Porterville, Rebecca's dad stopped in front of Marian's house and helped her out of the car with the soundly sleeping Ethan.

Marian looked at Rebecca with tears in her eyes. "Oh, Rebecca, how can I ever thank you for taking care of Ethan through all this horrible experience? And how can I make it up to you that you had to go through it?"

Startled, Rebecca thought, How weird that she thinks it's her fault that it happened, and I've been thinking it was my fault. She couldn't think of a good answer. At last she said, "I'll come by and see Ethan tomorrow, if that's okay."

Tremulously Ethan's mother said, "Of course it is. I'll see you tomorrow then."

As they drove away, Rebecca was still wired, unable to stop talking and relax until her father turned the corner of their street and she saw the lights of their house. Inside, while her mother bustled around heating up soup and making the guest-room bed for Bones, Rebecca picked up the telephone. When it was answered at the other end, she said softly, "Dani? It's me." And then, for the first time since she had been kidnapped, she broke down and wept.

That was Friday night. Over the weekend Rebecca felt as though she talked more than she ever had in her life. She and Bones spent a couple of hours at the police station with Sergeant Van Kerelin, going over the same ground they'd already covered earlier and trying to piece together the rest of the story.

The police had decided, without any real evidence, that the hang-up phone calls Rebecca had answered at Ethan's house were made by Mr. Underwood. Van Kerelin thought that Ethan's father had wanted to kidnap the little boy when he was away from the house, both to make it easier for himself and to reduce the number of possible witnesses.

Rebecca learned from her parents and then again from the police what Marian had told them about her former husband. The more she heard, the more she felt they had been very lucky that he hadn't done anything worse to her and Ethan.

It was hard for Rebecca to sort out her feelings, now that it was all over. Of course she was overwhelmed with relief that the ordeal had come to an end and they were all safe at home. She thought Mr. Underwood must have been a much sicker person than anyone had realized, and certainly that was sad. But what bothered her was that secretly she was glad he was dead. It's horrible to be happy that he got killed, she thought, but I am. At least he can never come after Ethan or me again.

Rebecca was surprised when Terry Milman, the social worker from school, appeared at the police station. Sergeant Kerelin explained that sometimes the police asked Terry to consult with them about cases that involved young victims of crimes. Terry and Rebecca sat down in a small office and talked for a while. Then Terry said, "You must be relieved that Mr. Underwood is dead."

Automatically Rebecca began to protest, but soon she found herself not only agreeing that she was indeed relieved but explaining in halting sentences how guilty she felt. The whole thing had been her fault; if she hadn't gotten into his car in the first place with Ethan, it never would have happened.

Just talking these things out with a sympathetic listener helped a lot. By the time they emerged from the office, Rebecca felt much better. It certainly would have been wiser not to have gone along with Ethan's father's wishes. But at least she'd been there for Ethan. What if he'd been kidnapped all by himself? As she left, Terry said, "If you want to talk about this again, just stop by my office at school anytime."

"Thanks," Rebecca told her, "maybe I will."

Meanwhile, people had been making a lot of phone calls and having a lot of discussions about Bones. Rebecca was determined that whatever was decided, Bones shouldn't have to go back to St. Ignatius. And it turned out that he wasn't there because he'd committed any crimes. He'd been sent to the school because he had no family to live with, and he hadn't gotten along with the foster parents in Newburgh.

Around noon on Sunday Kathy Delarra and her son Joe came over and everyone gathered around the Harpers' kitchen table. Kathy had a solution to Bones's situation: She suggested that he should come and live with her and attend Porterville High School. Now that Joe, the youngest of her four sons, had moved into his own apartment, she was alone in a large house and there was plenty of room. "I really want to do this," Kathy said. "I miss having a teenage boy around the house."

Later, as Rebecca and Bones walked over to visit Ethan, Bones said, "So, Rebecca, what do you think? About me living at this Mrs. Delarra's house?"

Rebecca turned to look at him. She hadn't been able to read his reaction to the idea when Kathy presented it, and she was a little surprised that he was asking her advice. "I think it's great," she said enthusiastically. "In fact, it's perfect! Kathy's really nice, and she's been lonely—I mean, she raised four sons, and her husband died a few years ago from cancer or something. And she's pretty easygoing, she wouldn't give you a hard time."

"That part sounds fine," Bones said slowly. "But what about school?"

"Do you mean are there any other black kids and will you fit in?" When Bones nodded, she went on seriously, "Yes, there are other black kids, but not very many. I don't think it would be a problem. Nobody at school seems to pay any attention to stuff like that." She paused and looked straight into his eyes. "But of course, I'm not black—I can only tell you how it seems from my point of view. I think you should give it a try."

After a moment Bones said, "I guess I will." Then with a wry grin he added, "No matter what, it'll beat St. Ignatius."

Ethan was delighted to see them, and Rebecca was happy to see that he was back to his normal cheery self. He was still getting over the flu, though, so they didn't stay long. As she walked them to the door, Mrs. Underwood said she planned to stay home from work the next day— Rebecca thought she wasn't ready to let Ethan out of her sight yet. But they arranged that Rebecca would start baby-sitting again on Tuesday.

At school on Monday Rebecca felt like a celebrity. Photos of her and Bones had appeared in the Sunday paper, and everybody wanted to hear all about the kidnapping and how they got away. It was fun to be the center of attention, even though Rebecca knew it wouldn't last very long.

Between second and third periods Andy Hollister caught up with her in the hall. "Glad to see you back, Rebecca," he said with a smile. "We were all worried about you."

He's still as handsome as ever, Rebecca thought in a detached way. Aloud she said, "Well, thanks, Andy."

Persisting, he said, "Are you free for lunch? I thought we could go down and grab a sandwich at the deli."

Rebecca couldn't help feeling a flicker of satisfaction. "No, sorry, I'm meeting someone."

An hour or so later she and Dani were standing by the doors of the cafeteria, waiting for Bones. At last she saw his lanky form striding along the hall toward them. "Sorry I'm late," he said. "I got lost."

"No problem," Rebecca told him. "Dani, this is Bones."

"I'm really glad to meet you," Dani said earnestly. "Rebecca is my best friend and, well, I'm glad she's back."

Bones gave her a slightly embarrassed smile, and the three of them went to join the food line. Before long they were sitting at a long table and Bones was telling yet again how it had happened that he was at the cabin and how he and Rebecca had escaped with Ethan. Rebecca listened as her friends peppered him with questions. Then Al Jenkins made a joke she didn't catch and Bones leaned back, roaring with laughter. It's nice to hear him sound so relaxed, Rebecca thought. Everything's going to work out fine.

"So, Rebecca, is Ethan okay now?" Dani asked. "Do you have to baby-sit this afternoon?"

Rebecca grinned at her friend. "No, I'm free today!" she said. "What do you want to do?"